NeW FicTIOn

CHILDREN'S CAROUSEL

Edited by

Steph Park-Pirie

First published in Great Britain in 2004 by
NEW FICTION
Remus House,
Coltsfoot Drive,
Peterborough, PE2 9JX
Telephone (01733) 898101
Fax (01733) 313524

SB ISBN 1 85929 116 3

FOREWORD

When 'New Fiction' ceased publishing there was much wailing and gnashing of teeth, the showcase for the short story had offered an opportunity for practitioners of the craft to demonstrate their talent.

Phoenix-like from the ashes, 'New Fiction' has risen with the sole purpose of bringing forth new and exciting short stories from new and exciting writers.

The art of the short story writer has been practised from ancient days, with many gifted writers producing small, but hauntingly memorable stories that linger in the imagination.

I believe this selection of stories will leave echoes in your mind for many days. Read on and enjoy the pleasure of that most perfect form of literature, the short story.

Parvus Est Bellus.

CONTENTS

THE LONELY PRINCESS
John J Allan

The king and queen of Senockia were very unhappy. Only that morning the queen had been delivered of their seventh child and it was another daughter. They longed for a son and here they were with seven daughters.

They were particularly devastated because the royal physician had told them that the queen could have no more children. And so the terrible truth crushed in on them. They would never have a son and heir to inherit the kingdom.

All the six previous princesses had been named after precious stones. The eldest was called Diamond, then Emerald, Sapphire, Ruby, Opal and Turquoise. By the time that the seventh and youngest princess had arrived the only name that anyone could think of was Rhinestone.

And she was so christened. It never sounded right and the young princess hated the name. It reminded her of her relatives in Eculand and she didn't like them at all. They were all red and very fat. Over the years, no matter how she protested, her name was abbreviated and to everyone she became Princess Rhine. This she disliked even more.

As the youngest princess grew up it became very apparent to everyone that she would never be a beauty. She was thin. Skinny was the word they used behind her back. She had a long neck, a small head and a rather prominent nose on which were balanced large, horn-rimmed spectacles.

Her father, the king, when he deigned to notice her at all, was heard to say to the queen, 'Our Rhine's growing into an ugly duckling.'

Princess Rhine knew she was plain but she consoled herself with the fact that she knew she was beautiful inside.

The years passed and the king grew more and more absent-minded and shut himself away to play with his train set. He could hardly remember who anyone was, least of all Princess Rhine. He couldn't remember who the queen was and when she came into his room, would shout, 'More logs for the fire!'

This upset the queen who got used to being mistaken for a servant but she did object to being thought of as the man who looked after the fires, for that was the lowliest job in the entire castle.

Once or twice a week the castle burst into activities as Rhine's six sisters got ready to go out to balls or parties. They were much in demand because they were all so beautiful, but invitations never came for Princess Rhine. Nobody wanted such a plain princess at their parties. Hairdressers and dressmakers would scurry between the six princesses.

Everywhere in the castle was confusion but when the princesses left for their particular engagements, Princess Rhine would retire to her little room at the top of the tallest turret. Although very lonely, Princess Rhine consoled herself with her little friends, the tiny animals and wild birds, that came to visit her. They would bring her presents of nuts and flowers and even their newly born babies for her approval. The princess also had the most wonderful view of the surrounding countryside with its lakes and wild fowl. The pine forest stretching away into the blue distance where it met the snow covered mountains.

One day while doing her tapestry feeling sad and alone, she looked out of the window and there on the edge of the lake stood a young man looking up at her window. He was very handsome and was wearing a tunic and hose with calf length boots, all in dazzling white. Fair, almost white curly hair was set off by a brilliant bright smile. Every day as soon as she awoke, she would rush to the window and he was always there looking at her. She became obsessed and determined to meet him.

One evening, while everyone was rushing around getting dinner ready, she slipped unnoticed out of the back door, ran across the yard and down the path to the lakeside where he was waiting.

Breathless, she confronted him.

'I'm Prince Avion,' he said, smiling that wonderful smile.

'I'm Princess Rhinestone,' she said apologetically, 'everyone calls me Rhine.'

He shook his head. 'That's not a pretty enough name for a Princess,' he exclaimed, 'I shall call you Irana, Princess Irana.'

Princess Rhine thought this was the most wonderful name she had every heard. From now on she would be Princess Irana.

'Are you happy Irana?' the prince enquired.

'I am now,' she smiled happily up at him.

'Are you lonely, Irana?' he asked.

'Not anymore,' she said.

'Come then, come with me,' and with her hand gently held in his, she found herself skimming across the surface of the lake. Up . . . up . . . up . . . high above the castle, over the pine forests, on upwards towards the snow covered mountains.

Looking around her, Irana found that she and Avion were leading a vast arrow formation of swans. Avion, Prince of the Swans and his Princess Irana were leading his people to the warm lands in the south.

BILLY BOY
Michelle Hinton

Rain was lashing down on the window, it was thundering and lightning. The trees were nearly uprooted because of the gale-force winds and there was Billy sitting at his desk doing his English homework. It was better than being outside in the storm and it was definitely a bad storm.

'Billy, Billy over here Billy,' whispered a voice.

'What was that voice I just heard, where is it coming from?' said Billy. He looked around the room. He could not see anybody. 'It must be my imagination,' he said and back to the books he went.

'Billy, Billy I am over here, look at me you stupid boy before I tear all your boring homework up,' said the voice.

'No way am I imagining that voice, something or someone is in my room.'

Suddenly all the books lifted off Billy's desk and they began flying around the room.

'Mum, Mum, help me Mum!' shouted Billy.

'Your mum cannot hear you Billy so stop shouting for help,' replied the voice.

'Leave me alone, leave me alone,' cried Billy.

'I am not going to leave you alone Billy boy, I want something that you have and it belongs to me,' said the voice.

'Where are you? I cannot see you, I don't know what you want!' cried Billy.

'Give me what I want Billy boy and I will go away!' replied the voice.

'Show yourself to me then and I will try and help you!' said Billy. Billy's eyes were wide open like an owl's. Beads of sweat were trickling down his face, he was petrified, he feared for his life.

'Shut your eyes Billy boy and count to ten. When you open them, you will see your worst nightmare,' said the voice.

'OK I will do it, one, two, three, four, five . . .' stammered Billy.

'Count faster scaredy cat,' shouted the voice.

'. . . six, seven, eight, nine, ten,' said Billy. Billy slowly opened his eyes and he wished he had kept them closed. Standing upside down on his bed was this *thing*. It had seven legs, one arm with two hands, a huge bald head and three eyes and a tiny mouth. All of a sudden the *thing* started laughing a horrible cackling kind of laugh.

'Do you like what you see Billy boy? Do you? Do you? Answer me stupid!' cackled the *thing*.

'No I think you are ugly, what are you? What do you want?' said Billy. Billy's heart was racing, his face was pale like a white tin of paint, his whole body was trembling with fright.

'I want your . . . give me what I want Billy boy and I will go away,' said the *thing*.

Billy started to feel terribly sick. He felt like he was going to faint. 'Tell me what you want Thing, I want to make you go away!' screamed Billy.

'Do not raise your voice at me Billy boy,' shouted the thing as it started spinning on his head. Close your eyes Billy boy and count to ten,' ordered the thing.

'OK anything, I will do it. One, two, three, four, five, six,' said Billy.

'Not so fast stupid, slow down,' said the thing.

'Seven, eight, nine, ten - now what do you want me to do?' asked Billy.

'Keep your eyes closed Billy boy, raise your arms slowly and put your hands on your head,' laughed the thing.

Billy's eyes were shut like glue. He slowly began to raise his arms and his hands reached his head. He felt weird, a cold feeling overtook him. 'Aaaaaaagh!' screamed Billy.

'Billy, Billy, what on earth are you screaming at?' said Billy's mum as she rushed into his bedroom.

'My hair, the thing took my hair, I have got no hair Mum, I am bald,' cried Billy.

'Oh Billy have you been watching your scary movies again? Your aunty Mable cut your hair today,' laughed Billy's mum as she closed Billy's bedroom door.

ROBERT
Peter Asher

The train moved off and stopped. It wasn't the points or the possibility of head on collision round the bend that held it, but the hand of Fate. All on board were in Fate's hand - and they knew it.

The passengers on this train were not happy travellers. Fate's hand let go a moment and went round the front of the train, where, being attached to Fate's arm, it placed itself, palm down and drummed Fate's fingers on the book of Fate - or rather Fate's Book of Captain Flat Worm stories.

Fate's eye placed itself on a level with the train while the other eye closed tightly to give more concentrated effort to the one seeing eye. 'If I was older I could have an electric one of these,' Fate remarked.

'Yes, and while your dad's wiring it up, he might even wire a switch for your brain when he does the *on* switch for the train. Or maybe just the one switch that would do for both.'

To this reply - no way by the way to speak to Fate - came another reply from the top of the carriage a carriage's length behind the reply from the first carriage. It replied, 'No brain to wire it to.'

'Are you ready?' yawned Mum, idly flicking the pages of a child's comic as she lay on the floor down line from Fate.

'Baby Kenneth's just told me he's sick of waiting for Nelly to get hurt.'

Fate angrily heaved himself up on his arms and became Poorly Boy. 'He never cos he dun't talk to you, only me and he doesn't say *hurt*, only *deaded.*'

'No he doesn't clever - and don't say *deaded* it's ignorant,' contradicted Mum, while correcting Poorly Boy's diction. She turned the page and got to the exciting bit where Captain Flat Worm (he of the big Fate's Annual fame from earlier,) smote the Wicked Ladybird with a series of the usual deft Captain Flat Worm smites. 'Any young rabbit who's of an age when he's able to take computer lessons every second Tuesday is old enough to use *hurt* instead of the rather baby rabbitish *deaded.*'

Poorly Boy stood, clenching his tiny fists all fuss and temper and glared at Mum. 'He's not going computering till Uncle Peter comes and till then he'll do as he's told and even after then he'll do as he's told. So if I ses he ses *deaded*, then he ses deaded!'

Mum sighed and pushing the comic aside, gave in and lay her cheek flat on the carpet, Baby Kenneth an arm's length to her right.

'Okay, tell me when you want us to start our emergency drill to save Nelly and Little Sheeps from the train crashing into the tunnel.'

'No no, no!' stormed Poorly Boy. 'You're deliberately getting it wrong. There's not going to be a crash in it. Nelly and Little Sheeps are going to get knocked off before it, because they're on the roofs but won't go through! I airplaned all that before.'

'Explained,' corrected Sue airily.

'That as well,' corrected Poorly Boy.

Poorly Boy, Mum and the two Team members who were endangered species, plus Baby Kenneth were practising their 'disaster response drill' as Mum called it. Poorly Boy called it *crash plastering* as in plastering wounds up after crashing. They did this drill periodically whenever Poorly Boy felt the Team needed a refresher course in watching him lose his temper. He wouldn't have seen it this way, preferring it to be a making sure everybody knew what to do if there was an accident or disaster. Actually though, the former description fitted better as if anyone was on the verge of disaster or accident it was Poorly Boy by falling over something in rage. He really did expect a lot from the Team - and Mum.

'You're far too tough with the Team - you bully them.'

'No I dun't at all Mum. You've seen on tele how in those movies when bridges fall down and airplanes lose their wings - *all* the rescuers say lots of things to each nuvers when they're busy rescuing. They talk *all* the way through the saving of people's lives. I want my Team to be able to rescue while talking all the time as well.'

Sue giggled, rolled over on her back and informed Poorly Boy that real life wasn't like the movies and the best rescuers keep their mouths shut; just get on and do it. But - of course Poorly Boy knew different as today he was in one of those splendid, knowing different to everyone else moods that five-year-olds (and the rest of us) have at times.

This morning's drill had Nelly and Little Sheeps sat astride the roof of Poorly Boy's push along train. The tunnel, seemingly bent on cutting off their heads, was to be thwarted in its nefarious deed by a derailment involving Mum's finger just before the tunnel entrance.

'If you don't derail us safely and in comfort before we're beheaded *I'll* never speak to you again,' warned Nelly quietly into Poorly Boy's ear as he lay beside her about to move the train off.

'And I promise on Nocky's knock knees I'll never make you laugh again at nasty and funny things I say, about Nelly and Mr Crumble Bee being in love, if you kill me,' threatened Little Sheeps, looking from the rear of Poorly Boy's ear.

'Don't worry you two sillies,' he assured, facing down line at Mum, still on her back unaware of this exchange as she bounced her Baby Kenneth about in the air above her; arms stretched full length upwards, holding his paws.

'They're having a great time aren't they?' observed Little Sheeps.

'You wait till Mum's finger gets run over and you come safely off the roof, parashusted down in my hand. Baby Kenneth'll bawl his tail sore with sitting on it crying!' Poorly Boy thought this remark very clever and didn't catch Little Sheeps and Nelly looking at one another with very dry looks indeed. Not until he turned their way anyway. 'You do trust me don't you?' He'd seen something in their eyes.

'No!' they said in rare and absolute unanimity.

Poorly Boy started to push engine and train forward.

A fairly quiet town with reasonably decent villains and a population of ordinary troublesome folk; neither too bad or too good, does have its moments. Peter had reported on many of these good people's moments. How their lives became newsworthy whenever their lives became like the lives of their readers - with loves going wrong or events taking over. Their readers and indeed, their reporters.

Peter had reported so many moments and seen things he'd not like his young nephew, his sister nor his brother-in-law to see. But how was he going to avoid this moment - for two reasons. Firstly, he didn't want Poorly Boy to see what looked like a car stranded on the traffic island just now. Secondly - ah secondly - he felt too wretched simply to walk. His heart, as they say, was heavy, too heavy for the fattest of Cupids to heave around.

The light green gate with the safety catch as safe as Poorly Boy wanted everyone to think it was, snecked behind him. Peter braced himself for the fiction he wasn't about to write but tell. As he approached the green door in thought, he remembered to start limping slightly. Either his nephew or Baby Kenneth must have seen him coming (they'd be expecting him at this time on every second Tuesday anyway). Which of them saw him first, Peter couldn't tell but Poorly Boy's distant gleeful voice sounded from inside a second before Baby Kenneth's blue, floppy ears flopped through the letterbox from inside out. Poorly Boy's voice much louder now, followed the ears from inside the same oblong hole in the door. 'Want a bun Uncle Peter, wivs a teacup before we go? We were going to have a train crash but Baby Kenneth got scared Nelly would get hurt - and when Little Sheeps started to make fun of him saying there was no use him falling in love with Nelly because she was all gooey about Crumble Bee, he ran away into the hall just about the same time I saw you coming from the window which was just after the clock said you should be here. Door's not locked, come on.' Poorly Boy and Baby Kenneth dragged Peter through a partly opened door with a bit of a knee bump and shoulder thump, but nothing too serious to dampen Peter's momentarily uplifted spirits at the exuberance of the welcome.

'Least somebody still loves me,' he chuckled.

'Oh cors we do Uncle Peter - we loves yous because you's the bestest reporter and poet the office has ever seen. In't that so Baby Kenneth?'

To which the young, blue rabbit's ear flapped in exuberant affirmation with such gusto he flew out of Poorly Boy's hand right up at Peter's face and kissed him before dropping down to polish his hero's trainers.

'What adulation, what fame!' enthused Peter, even against his underlying sorrowful and morose mood. 'I've a bit of a bad leg today,' he continued.

'How you do that? Do you want an appointment with Mr Crumble Bee? He's not got anyone to do for a while and he's real good at legs - remember Little Sheeps?'

Peter did remember how Crumble Bee, the talk of every dying flower in the garden, had recommended Little Sheeps be kept moving as aid to setting his broken legs after Poorly Boy had tossed him on the floor in temper.

'No thanks,' Peter declined, 'It'll go when the weather turns warmer; just rheumatism from an old football injury.'

'Mr Crumble Bee's great with injured footballs,' said Poorly Boy persistently, 'he squishes them and puts them to rest.'

'I see, so they're limp, is that it?' enquired Peter.

'They don't limp Uncle Peter,' came the reply, 'not in bed anyway.'

Sue was smiling like someone who was looking forward to being five-year-old-less and alone with Little Sheeps for a few hours. 'What's this about injured ex-footballers - you are still going to the office with Poorly Boy aren't you Peter.' Her face dropped as the dark possibility he might not be suddenly grabbed hold of it, pulling it downwards.

'Er-yes, of course - only we'll be going in my car and not parking it up here in the garage drive as we usually do. We'd better go the direct way also, so I've as little gear changing work as possible with the poor old foot.' He turned to Poorly Boy, 'That'll mean we won't be going by the traffic island I'm afraid old son,' he smiled, weakly apologetic.

'Awe Uncle Peter - I love rounding the roundabout - but if your foot's sick I don't mind - course I don't!' he said cheerfully. 'Maybe by tonight your foot will feel better and we can come home that way.'

That was okay with Peter, although he didn't say so. By evening the police should have cleared what appeared at a swift, horrified glance to be a battered old Vauxhall with a teddy bear trapped in the rear door by its arm and stranded way up on the island flower beds.

Peter was pleased with himself. For long enough, every second Tuesday when Peter and Clive the photographer had a day off, talking over future projects, Poorly Boy and him walked the shortish distance to the office if it was fine via the traffic island. Poorly Boy loved to spend a few minutes both ways watching the traffic while clutching Baby Kenneth and Nelly; his usual accompanists on the office venture. Those hours at the newspaper headquarters spent with the office girls - for lucky Poorly Boy and his two team members mused Peter - while the girls gave the blue rabbit computer lessons, and the reporter, together with his photographer mulled professional matters over in an adjacent room.

Poorly Boy had understood fully how the poorly leg and or foot meant they'd have to go by car today - the shortest possible way.

'Let's have a final check. Knowing you you'll get there and find you've forgotten Baby Kenneth's dummy or something.' Mum was used to this. So Poorly Boy remembered he'd forgotten Baby Kenneth's carrot dummy and Mum went away to reappear with a baby pre-prepared one out of a child's luncheon pack of baby carrots.

'Good thing I thought to check.' Poorly Boy jauntily shoved the dummy, blue rabbit nosewards. 'Aren't I a good organoser?' he sighed as if exasperated at everyone's inefficiency. Nelly too made sure she wasn't left behind with the sardonic Little Sheeps on the railway track as she loved to be spoilt by the office girls and certainly didn't fancy a Spartan day stranded and railway carriaged with a sarcastic woolly sheep.

Peter hobbled theatrically to the car assisted by Nurse Nelly and Poorly Boy's arm holding her around Uncle Peter's knee.

'Oh, isn't it painful!' Sue remarked, her younger brother flashing a glance at her unduly ironical tone. 'Shouldn't you have it X-rayed?'

'No Mum,' Poorly Boy replied on behalf of his uncle as he opened the car door for him while Nelly held Peter's knee, presumably propping him up as he leant on the roof. 'Uncle doesn't want none of those because they burn you like when I put Little Sheeps too near the toaster. You said so yourself that he smelt like they'd X-rayed his ears and forgot to switch the machine off.'

'Go on you lot, keep out of my hair for a few hours,' chided Sue. She waved them away, wondering what really was wrong with her young brother - as if she didn't know. She'd seen that look on his face a few times and knew what was behind it and it wasn't a leg, unless a far more shapely one than Peter's . . .

Peter was just about to wipe his mental brow with his brilliant imitation of a man with either/or poorly leg or/either poorly foot and pat his inventiveness and acting ability on the cerebral back, when he turned the corner onto the short journey to the office. A huge yellow diversion sign on account of a student's rag week procession it wanted him to know about was coming his way. It met him at the roadside to inform him of its decision to re-route the traffic via the roundabout. Peter groaned. 'What's it say, Uncle Peter?' Poorly Boy exclaimed. 'Well isn't that funny Uncle! You'd never believe it would you unless Nelly, me and Baby Kenneth were here to see it with you, would you?'

Like a man deflated by many defeats who's lost his will even to be defeated, Peter followed the detour.

'Uncle Peter,' came the voice, 'What do the students want rags for?' Peter motored doomily on.

'That daft man in the van just tooted us Uncle Peter. What's he do that for we're not in his way. Aren't some people incondurate?'

'Indeed they are - and some daft road signs,' replied Peter enigmatically, closing moment by moment on the inevitable.

'Awe, Uncle Peter - look at that crashed car on the flower bed with those gnomes and dwarves all around it. In't that a sight!'

Peter almost lost control of nerves and car. Fortunately the roundabout wasn't a busy one - and at a more studied pace than earlier - the *crashed* car appeared decidedly more bent by wear and age than by collision, with its attendant dwarves, gnomes and elves scattered around the island. And was that or not was that Clive with a Robin Hood hat on taking photographs?

'Uncle Peter - in't that your friend Clive who buys me a drink at the office, waving us to pull over and do something about that poor, poor teddy trapped by his arm in the car's back door?'

So many questions for one day. Peter didn't care anymore. He pulled in behind a parked police car; one officer at the radio, one directing proceedings amongst the gnomes and Robin on the traffic island. Peter didn't in truth feel at all well - it was his head not his leg that hurt. He sat wondering what to do as Robin Clive came towards him. Nelly and Baby Kenneth were gazing at the sight through the window with a silent and opened mouthed Poorly Boy. Silence and the open mouth were usually a bad combination with Poorly Boy - presaging the fruition of some master plan or other.

'Morning Pete. Morning Nelly, Baby Kenneth and you my lad.' Clive brightly upbeat, rested an elbow and forearm on the open car window ledge. 'Coleman phoned me to get down here sharpish and get photos. Suppose he got you to come too?' It wasn't turning out the way Peter had planned it at all.

'Nelly finks we ought to go and rescue that teddy bear Uncle Peter.' Peter shut his eyes tightly and squeezed the gear lever more tightly.

'What a great idea Poorly Boy,' said Clive enthusiastically, 'the poor thing does look miserable and woebegone.'

'If we get him out alive we can take him back to the children he belongs to - once Nelly says Mr Crumble Bee has operated on him and made him better,' suggested Poorly Boy.

Clive opened the passenger door and helped Poorly Boy out the rear seat. 'You stay there Peter - you don't look at all well. We'll handle this and I'll get clicking.'

Poorly Boy, Clive, Nelly and Baby Kenneth trotted over the road to the island. Peter watched, making no effort to follow. This was not like him; the exuberant witty one - the rightful aider and abetter in Poorly Boy escapades.

The passenger door opened and Geraldine slipped in, her hand alighting on his knee. 'Peter, I'm so sorry. Last night, forgive me.' Geraldine; newest member from out of town on the reporting staff. Geraldine, of the long golden hair. Geraldine of Peter's lost heart, walked across beside a beaming Peter to the operation scene.

'Geraldine's here to report, after Coleman phoned her. I'm at a loose end I guess - so can I help?' Peter asked sheepishly.

'Shush Uncle. Clive's given teddy some Vick to put him to sleep and I'm telling Clive how to get the trapped arm free.'

Peter felt and looked woebegone. God - he felt jealous. Geraldine knew and blinked a long, slow green-eyed blink and squeezed his hand reassuringly. Peter felt all at once quite content to stay out of this one.

One of the students with a big card hung round his neck pranced up to them. Robert bowed low and courtly in his medieval-come-gnome costume. Without a word he bent forward, kissed Poorly Boy on the head knelt before the trapped teddy; opened the door with a key - and let the teddy free. Poorly Boy, amazed, enthralled and hypnotised all at once, stood and felt his arms being gently folded about the teddy as Robert laid it by Poorly Boy's chest, Nelly still clutched in one hand and Baby Kenneth in the other, forming a cross. Robert stepped back as Poorly Boy knelt again. Robert bowed deeply from the waist with a fine sweep of his right arm, brushing the grass before him at his feet in front of Poorly Boy, with fingers and the feather in his hat. Then Robert unlocked the front door, wound the window down, smiled broadly, turned the ignition and amidst clouds of bangs and smoke of black - drove the car forwards. As it chugged, the smoke exhumed the strategically placed wooden planks hitherto unnoticed, protecting the flower bed from harm across the grass divide where one bed ended and another began; the other two tyres being on the close cropped remainder of the island. The scene was instantly returned to its virgin and unspoilt condition and everyone drifted - college, home, office or townwards.

Baby Kenneth's computer lesson was shared that Tuesday with his new friend, a teddy bear called Robert, whom Geraldine had fallen in love with. Baby Kenneth suggested she take him home to live with her and seeing as he was an expert with computers, he continued (for a time at least) to teach Baby Kenneth every second Tuesday.

THE PINK FEATHER
Patricia Smith

'Of course I was the belle of the ball; what everybody was looking at, round and round under the shimmering chandeliers. Rivers of champagne, mountains of caviar and those delicate little ices; didn't get home until four in the morning. Even I looked a bit bedraggled, but I was ready for the next time'.

'Oh listen to her,' sighed the headband, 'will she never stop talking about it; one ball that's all she went to. From the way she goes on you'd think that a feather could stand up on its own. Everybody knows it was me; that I made the outfit, just the right shade of cream and heavy satin, such a good fabric. If I hadn't stayed in place through all the dances and I didn't move once let me tell you, where would that silly pink feather have been? On the floor, trampled underfoot; that's where.'

'Come now. Come now!' cajoled the fox fur, looking down his long snout. 'We've been through this time and time again. You both had your parts to play. Feather would not have held her place without you Headband, I grant you that, but you have to admit that you would have been rather uninteresting on your own without her.'

'What would you know?' retorted Headband. 'You didn't see anything; a maid took you away when we came in and you weren't brought out again until it was time to leave, so you know nothing about it.'

'Quite so,' confirmed Feather, for once agreeing, 'he's all moth-eaten and nobody would want him now and he'll probably soon be illegal and he has glass eyes and he's always pretending to be better than us.'

'Do calm down both of you. You are correct, I was not in the ballroom, but I can use my imagination. You forget that I have the greater intellect. I was real once, I was alive; not like the rest of you. Pieces of frippery; that is all you are.'

'Well I come from an ostrich and a big one at that, bigger than you ever were,' flounced Feather, 'so there.'

'But my dear, you were dyed.' This came from Headband who seemed to think that because hers was the colour of a foodstuff that somehow that made her natural.

'Dyed, well I was like dyed; tied in a knot and dyed. *Died.*' This came from a small, lilac and lime green bundle scrunched up in the corner of the box.

'I think you will find that is spelt *Dyed,*' said Fox-fur, again looking disdainful, 'what did I do to end up here with such ill-educated accessories?'

'Who are you calling uneducated? Can I remind you that T-shirt and I were at the LSE. Hey, perhaps we don't remember much about it; just the sitting in. But we were there; changing the world. Not parasites kept in luxury by the sweat of the working classes.'

'I suppose you were needed for elementary arithmetic,' Fox-fur muttered to himself, 'education went sadly downhill in the sixties.'

'In our day you would have been pearls; nothing less. Not some nasty pieces of old wood,' sneered Headband who could be quite hurtful sometimes.

'Beads and I are really like down, OK so you don't put anymore on us,' moaned T-shirt who had absorbed so many illegal substances over the years that he found it almost impossible to cope with any emotion. 'Yeah, we think it's really bad karma being in this box; like we are never going to get out.'

'I do wish you would speak correctly and enunciate clearly,' sighed Fox-fur, 'the King's English has never been so abused. Why people do not segregate the decades in storage. I fail to understand.'

'You should keep up more up to date Fox-fur,' ventured Headband, a little nervous at having found something to correct after all these years, 'it's Queen now.'

'The queen; she's a man? Heavy,' gasped T-shirt who had trouble following any line of thought.

Feather had been preening and fluffing herself up in a small fragment of mirror, 'I think only very important accessories would have been dyed and I'm a very special pink. I had to be just the right shade for the dress, but of course it would have been nothing without me. I was the belle of the ball, what everybody was looking at; round and round under the shimmering chandeliers.'

'Oh no, not again. Please not again,' shrieked Headband, Fox-fur, T-shirt and Beads almost in unison.

'I will consider my plan of escape,' said Fox-fur grandly, 'I am sure that we would all welcome being free.'

'Free, right on, I'm not into bread man,' replied T-shirt.

'Money is an artificial construct of the capitalist system,' intoned Beads.

Just as they were all worrying that another half-remembered pseudo-Marxist-Leninist diatribe was coming their way, the loft door opened.

'Come on William; Mother will be back soon and then we'll have to stop for tea. Look at this junk. You take that mangy fur thing and be the trapper.'

'Mangy fur thing, are you addressing me young man?' asked Fox-fur haughtily, but of course Joe could not hear him. The others smirked.

'That bit of old cloth can be part of my Red Indian head-dress.'

'I am not old, merely a certain age,' sighed Headband, but nonetheless she was pleased to get back something of her past role, 'after all, I expect he will be a warrior chief,' she mused.

'You can use these beads to buy Manhattan from me,' instructed Joe.

Whilst Beads was considering his response to being instrumental in such an important business transaction and wondering whether he would become an investment banker, William was looking into the far corner of the box.

'We'll need something to clean off the war paint; bring along that purple and snot-coloured rag as well.'

'Yeah, rag week; that's really far out,' said T-shirt.

'What about me, you must need me!' cried Feather. The others hoped so, for, even though she could be very annoying, she was their friend and they all wanted to be free.

'You'll need a feather,' said William, 'Indians always had feathers.'

'A pink feather?' Joe was not pleased. 'I can't be a proper Red Indian wearing such a girlie colour; everybody will look at me.'

It is quieter now, but Feather does not notice. She has forgotten about her friends. The mirror is still there and it never seems to tire of hearing her story. 'Of course, I was the belle of the ball, what everybody was looking at.'

THE YAWRON'S MAGICAL MUSIC
Carol Ann Darling

To the far north, where the cold winds blow and the snow falls deep on the mountain tops, the Yawron, meaning *haunting song*, would sit for hours playing his delightful music. He would start early in the morning, as soon as the sun rose from behind the mystical mountains and continue until the sun had set and darkness was descending at dusk. Then and only then, would he rest, composing in his magical mind, tunes for the following day. The musical notes drifted through his dreams. Each day the sweet music was different. He never played the same tune twice.

All the dwellers of the surrounding countryside knew of the Yawron's beautiful, alluring calling but danger lurked from where the music flowed. The dwellers longed to see the Yawron but to fall for and be lured by the Yawron's pipes and strings had ended in peril for every attempt to visit him. So the dwellers of all the nestled hamlets under the towering snowy peaks, where the Yawron lived, went about their daily lives humming and singing along, just enjoying the lilting, honeyed melodies of his concerts from a safe distance.

In the hamlet of Fjeldsang lived the pretty shop assistant Anglend. She worked hard from dawn to dusk in her papa's hamlet food store. As she served the customers, all day long she could hear the Yawron's soulful tunes *tripping over the mountains, through the streams, over the stones into Fjeldsang and out the other side.* She longed to climb the mountain path. Mesmerised, she would gaze out the shop window to the peaks above.

Seeing her watery eyes, her papa would say, 'It is dangerous Anglend!'

'You must not attempt the path, Anglend,' joined in her mama, 'it is said the music is just a tease, a promise of a happiness which can never be. It has caught the fancy of many a dweller and visitor to our Fjeldsang. Enticing them, they have never been seen again.'

'But Papa, Mama, it calls to me. Can't you hear my name? Anglend, Anglend, over and over the music calls. Just say you can hear it too!'

'No, my dear Anglend,' replied Papa, 'it calls to everyone. Every dweller hears their name. Even I hear my name. Lom, Lom, I hear it every day.'

'No Papa, it calls my name. Only my name, Anglend, comes *tripping over the mountains, through the streams, over the stones into Fjeldsang and out the other side.*'

Anglend struggled with her heart daily.

'I must visit the music. I must see the Yawron and sing along. Look Papa, I have written words to accompany the music,' pleaded Anglend.

'No, my little Anglend, you must not go. I forbid you. If you were to go, we would never see you again. The Yawron casts a spell. He is not to be approached. The fables say, he will never stop playing. He is cursed. He is bad, the Yawron. You must not go. Promise me, Anglend, promise me you will do as I say?' cried out Papa.

'But Papa!' sobbed Anglend.

'Anglend, I will hear no more. If you do not obey your papa, I will send you to stay with your grandmama many, many miles away, where the Yawron's music cannot be heard,' said Papa, with Mama's agreeing look.

At this Anglend knew she must do as she was instructed.

Year in, year out, Anglend continued to hear the trickling notes, dulcet on the mountain air. It was calling her name. It was promising pleasures and joy. It was offering serenity and harmony. And it was breaking her lonely heart. She longed to meet the Yawron. She desired to see him play. She cried tears of discontent for her dreams were of the Yawron and his passionate strumming sounds.

One afternoon, while working in Papa's store, she could no longer control her feelings. The music was playing her heart, caressing her face, tingling her legs and arms.

'Come to me Anglend. Come to me Anglend,' sighed the music, *tripping over the mountains, through the streams, over the stones into Fjeldsang and out the other side.* She could hear it. She could feel it. She would touch it. She *would* see the Yawron.

Anglend was running through the hamlet.

'Why are you in such a hurry, Anglend?'

'Anglend, does your papa know the way you are heading?'

'Why aren't you working in the store?' various dwellers did shout.

But Anglend did not reply. She just kept going, following the enchanting tones of jingling and jangling bells, pipes, harps and soft drumming.

She was on the mountain path. Her legs were aching with running so fast and her heart was banging. She had to stop for breath. The air was becoming thinner. The mountain path climbed steeply. The music was louder than she had ever heard it. A violin was sobbing as the bow swept the strings. It was too late to turn back. She couldn't face Papa and Mama. She would be in so much trouble. On and on, up and up, she climbed towards the towering peaks. Above the tree line, it became much colder. She snuggled into her coat. She was hungry. She hadn't thought to pack any food. The music was floating down to her. She had to carry on. The path was becoming narrower. The rocks were radiating pink and yellow. It was serene. It was so blissful. She felt she was in a heaven, a heaven on Earth.

Then there was a silence, a ghostly silence. All was grey. All was quiet. The music had ceased. It was dusk, time for the Yawron to rest and dreamily compose for the following day. But coming through the stony silence was a beautiful, angelic voice.

'Anglend, Anglend, you've come. For years I have been whispering in my music for you to come. I have been calling and calling you. But you didn't come, until now,' said the angelic voice.

'Is that you Yawron? Where are you? I can't see you,' pleaded Anglend.

'Yes, I am Yawron. I am invisible, Anglend. You cannot see me. You can only hear me. I can only become visible if you make a certain answer to me,' replied Yawron.

'Hhhow did you know my name, Yawron?' stuttered Anglend, 'and why are you invisible Yawron, why is that so?'

'A jealous troll called Tulla placed a spell on me. Tulla hated my music and my singing. She doomed me to the mountain tops with only berries that the birds would bring me to eat and snow water to drink. Tulla, the troll said, that only Anglend of Fjeldsang could make it to the top of this mountain to free me from her spell. That all others would perish in an attempt to find me. Tulla said that Anglend's dedication would be so great she would ignore all dangers and throw her life to the cold winds and deep snow and stand before me,' replied Yawron in a thankful voice.

'I had to come. I heard your lullabies. I heard your soul crying to the stars. I felt your blue skies, touched your rainy days. I empathised with your longing and I wanted to belong. I wanted to visit you but Papa kept saying no. He said all travellers on the mountain path to the Yawron's musical heart would perish. And then I could wait no longer. I ran and climbed and climbed. But I can't see you. I want to see you Yawron. I have to see your face. I must watch you play and help with the composing and playing of the instruments. Tell me how Yawron, tell me now.'

'Will you marry me Anglend? Say you will marry me. Only that now will break Tulla's spell. You cannot see me unless you first agree that you will marry me. Then I will be visible. Then you will see me and all the instruments,' replied Yawron.

'Yes Yawron, yes I will marry you,' shouted Anglend, as her voice echoed all around, *tripping over the mountains, through the streams, over the stones into Fjeldsang and out the other side.*

In an instant, there was a flash of brilliant white light and there stood Yawron. He was tall, wearing sunglasses and holding a harp, surrounded by many instruments, including drums, a violin, a piano, triangles and bells. He put his arms around Anglend.

'I love you Anglend. I called for you to come. I waited for your arrival and this answer for so long. You have saved me from a life of invisibility and given me the freedom to descend the mountain,' said Yawron thankfully.

'I love you too,' smiled Anglend, 'I have loved you for years. I loved you from afar. Now, I shall love you close.'

'It's time to dream and compose new songs for tomorrow. Look Anglend, the stars are beckoning. The moon is rising, brightening the dark. The music must play on tomorrow, even though Tulla's spell is broken.'

'Yes, Yawron,' agreed Anglend, 'the dwellers of Fjeldsang and surrounding countryside love your music. It must not stop.'

Early the next day, as the sun rose, the Yawron's music was to be heard as usual but full of interesting new rhythms and tempos, assisted by Anglend, who was to stay with Yawron forever.

It is said that Yawron and Anglend were married in the hamlet of Fjeldsang, with Papa's blessing, after he had scolded Anglend over and over. Apparently, he had heard Anglend's voice as it had echoed around the mountain tops and he had been fearfully worried. But now all was well. Tulla's spell was broken and the dwellers were free to climb the mountain path as in the days of many, many years ago, to pick berries and graze their sheep.

It is said, the music of Yawron and Anglend can still be heard as the melting snows trickle, making crystal streams and that the mountain streams are the tears of the Yawron and Anglend's happiness.

It is also said, that if you turn your ear to the far north, where the cold winds blow and the snow falls deep on the mountain tops, an angelic voice whispering *Anglend* can still be heard as it comes *tripping over the mountains, through the steams, over the stones into Fjeldsang and out the other side.*

Yes, yes, listen. I can hear it. Can you?

HILDA THE HEDGEHOG GETS PRICKLED
Jacqueline G Harris

One Friday, when the young Oak Town animals had finished school. They planned, on their way home, they would have some fun and go on an adventure at the weekend.

So when they arrived home, they told their mums and dads. There was baby squirrel, Harry the hedgehog and Billy Brock the badger. The fox cubs were too young.

The plan was to go to bed early Friday night. Then their mums pack them some sandwiches and some fresh spring water from the stream and they were going on a long walk.

Their parents agreed, but they would not let them stay out all night, because they thought they were too young. Mrs Squirrel asked Mr Fox if he would follow behind to make sure they were all right. He agreed to do so.

'As it is their first big adventure, I will,' he said.

The little ones went to bed at six o'clock. As they were going to get up at 7am the next day to set off on their adventure.

Mr Fox did not tell anyone what he was doing. So they did not get worried about them, and decided they could not go. Baby squirrel could not sleep, he was so excited. So he went onto the branch and told his mum.

She said, 'Just daydream and count acorns.'

'There's too many on the tree, Mummy,' he said.

'Not the ones on the tree,' Mrs Squirrel told him, 'pretend ones.'

'Alright!' replied baby squirrel.

So he went back to bed. He just relaxed and pretended to count acorns, and was soon fast asleep. Billy Brock went to sleep straight away. So did Harry the hedgehog. The fox cubs asked if they could go, but Mr and Mrs Fox said, 'No.'

So they curled up in a corner of the lair and sulked until they fell fast asleep.

Morning soon came, the three adventurers got dressed, had their breakfast and put their sandwiches in their backpacks. Also their spring water, in small bottles they had found in the wood. They said their goodbyes and kissed their mums. They met at the big sycamore tree near the squirrels and set off.

'Shall we go past Thunder's field?'

'Oh yes,' yelled baby squirrel.

'We'll have to go and see old Thunder and his friends.'

'We'll rest when you want to, baby squirrel,' Billy Brock told him.

'Alright,' was the reply.

The three little friends took their time and soon arrived at Thunder the horse's field. They could not see Thunder at first, but saw Frosty, Ella's foal.

'I will go and get him,' neighed Frosty.

Soon Thunder came galloping from the other end of the field.

'Why, hello there you three,' he whinnied.

'Where are you off to?'

'We're going to the meadow,' said the three furry friends.

'I am going to get my mum a flower,' said Harry.

'I'm going to get some ants,' said Billy.

Baby squirrel last of all said, 'I'm going to get some chestnuts for tea.'

'My, that sounds fun,' neighed Thunder. 'Good luck.'

'I've got to go now, I need a drink from the trough with all that galloping - see you then.'

The three set off on their quest.

Mr Fox was following in the distance, he did not let the three friends see him. He knew they were alright.

Billy, baby squirrel and Harry soon reached the meadow.

'We'll sit by this log and eat our sandwiches,' said Billy.

So they did.

'I enjoyed them,' said baby squirrel.

'So did I,' replied the other two.

Billy found his ants inside the log and put them in a paper bag he'd saved. Baby squirrel found a chestnut tree and got his chestnuts and put them in his backpack.

Then Harry gave a shout, 'I've found one!'

'What?' was the reply.

'A flower, it's a purple one with pointy leaves!'

So they were all happy, and set off back home with their gifts.

It was teatime around five o'clock when they arrived home. Billy gave the ants to his dad and told him they were to share with his mum. Baby squirrel emptied his backpack on the floor and the chestnuts fell out. He told his mum they were for her and his dad, but he would like just one.

'Of course,' laughed his mum.

Then Harry gave his mum the flower.

'Oh lovely,' and she thanked Harry.

'Do you like it then?' Harry asked.

'Oh I do, it's lovely Harry!'

'Have a smell, and see if it smells nice,' he replied.

'Ouch!' yelled Hilda.

'What's the matter Mum?' asked Harry.

'The flower prickled me!'

'Oh dear, I thought it was a special one for you.'

'Oh it is,' said his mum, 'it's lovely, but it is prickly.'

It was a thistle.

EMILY'S SECRET WISH
Mimie

Emily was four and a bit. The 'bit' was very important to Emily because when she was five she would be taller and then maybe, just maybe, her secret wish would come true and someone would want her for their bridesmaid.

For as long as she could remember she had wanted to be a bridesmaid. Her sister Jane, who was seven, had been a bridesmaid three times and Emily was so jealous. She so wanted to wear a pretty dress with little bows on, dainty shoes and flowers in her hair, but her mother always said the same thing. 'You are too little Emily, wait until you are older.'

Today was Saturday and Emily was going with her mum, dad and sister to the seaside for the day. It was a lovely warm day so they sat on the beach and made sandcastles and paddled in the sea and looked for pretty shells and stones to take home with them.

Emily was getting bored with this when suddenly she saw something blue and shiny between two rocks. She knelt down and pulled out the prettiest little blue stone you have ever seen.

'Look Mum,' she called excitedly, 'look what I've found.'

Everyone came to see what Emily was holding in her hands.

'Oh Emily,' said Mum, 'how lucky you are, you have found a fairy stone.'

'What's that?' asked Emily.

'Well,' said her mum, 'it is supposed to make your dreams come true. If you look carefully into the stone you will see a little fairy and if you tell her what you most wish for, it should come true.'

Emily was so excited and carefully wrapped the beautiful stone in her handkerchief to take home.

As soon as she got home Emily raced to her bedroom and unwrapped the stone. She carried it over to the window to get more light and then she looked into the middle of the stone, but no little fairy appeared but Emily thought she would make her wish anyway. So she closed her eyes and held the stone tightly in her hands and wished that she could be a bridesmaid.

The next day Emily waited eagerly in case the phone should ring, or a letter would come or someone would call asking her to be their bridesmaid, but nothing happened.

Emily didn't give up and every day she looked into the stone, closed her eyes and wished that she could be a bridesmaid, but she never saw the fairy and no one asked her to be their bridesmaid.

The weeks went by and Emily started to give up believing in the magic of the stone and one day when she was holding it in her hands to make her wish, she suddenly lost her temper.

'You stupid stone,' she shouted, 'you are not a fairy stone, you are just a silly old stone off the beach,' and she threw it under the bed and stamped off downstairs to have her breakfast.

Just as she had sat down at the table and dipped her spoon into her cornflakes, there was a ring at the front door and she heard her mum open it and start chatting to their next-door neighbour, Miss Pink. After a few minutes, Mum came into the room with Miss Pink and they both had big smiles on their faces.

'Emily,' said her mum, 'Miss Pink has something very special she wants to ask you.' Emily looked at Miss Pink and quickly swallowed the spoonful of cornflakes she had in her mouth.

'Emily dear,' said Miss Pink, 'something wonderful has happened, I have met a man at my computer classes and we have fallen in love and are going to get married.'

'That's nice,' said Emily wondering what it had to do with her.

'Well,' continued Miss Pink, 'I wondered if you would be my bridesmaid?'

Emily opened her mouth in disbelief and a few cornflakes fell out. 'What me?' she gasped, 'why do you want me?'

'Because you are just the right size and are such a pretty little girl,' said Miss Pink. 'I have two grown-up nieces who will be my two big bridesmaids and another little one of four, who is the daughter of my friend, but I need another little one to walk beside her. Will you do it for me?'

Would she be a bridesmaid? Emily couldn't believe her ears. 'Oh yes, yes!' she gasped. 'Yes please, I have always wanted to be a bridesmaid.'

Mum and Miss Pink beamed at her.

'Right,' said Miss Pink, 'we will have a lovely time together choosing your dress and shoes and getting flowers for your hair. I'm not getting married for quite a few weeks, so we will have plenty of time to get everything. I'll see you tomorrow and we can go to look for your dress.'

Emily was so excited that she couldn't finish her breakfast. She danced round and round the room singing, 'I'm going to be a bridesmaid,' over and over again at the top of her voice.

Suddenly, Emily remembered the fairy stone and ran to her bedroom and crawled under the bed and there in the corner she could see the little blue stone glowing in the dark. She picked it up and carried it to the window and said, 'You *are* a fairy stone because my wish has come true. I'm sorry I didn't believe in you,' and then she looked into the stone and there in the middle was a little fairy smiling at her. Emily blinked her eyes and when she looked again the fairy had disappeared, but Emily knew that she hadn't imagined it. She had seen the fairy and her wish had come true because she was going to be a bridesmaid.

So, if ever you are on the beach looking for shells and stones and you see a blue shiny stone hidden in the rocks, make sure that you pick it up and take it home, because you *may* have found a fairy stone and like Emily your secret wish *may* come true.

THE MONSTER AND THE MAGIC HAT
Joyce Walker

Once upon a time there was a monster that was so ugly he wanted a magic hat to make him invisible. So he went to the hat shop.

The man in the shop said, 'I have a fez with a tassel, a boater made of straw, a wide-brimmed sombrero that won't fit through the door. A pretty Easter bonnet, fit for a parade all decked out with chicks and bright yellow braid. A tartan Tam O'Shanter, a beret for a cat, but yesterday I sold right out of magic hats.'

The monster asked the shopkeeper where he might find one, but the shopkeeper did not know. This made the monster very angry and he stamped his feet so hard he made a hole in the floor and the shopkeeper, afraid that he might soon have no shop left at all said, 'You could try the old wizard who lives at the top of the hill.'

So the monster climbed and climbed till he reached to top of the hill and knocked on the door of the wizard's house.

When the wizard came to the door, the monster said, 'I really need a hat, it can be tall or thin or fat, pointed, round or flat, but not any kind of hat, it must be a magic hat.'

The wizard asked the monster why he wanted the magic hat and the monster said that he wanted to make himself invisible. The wizard took the hat from his own head and handed it to the monster. 'I can give you the hat,' he said, 'but I am so old that my magic doesn't work anymore. Perhaps if you go to Magic Town, my friend the magician will be able to help you.'

The monster thanked the wizard for his hat, put it on his head and took the bus to Magic Town. It took him a long time to get to Wand Street where the magician lived, but finally he reached the magician's door and knocked.

When the magician opened it he said, 'Please Mr Magician, can you give me some magic for the wizard's hat? I want to become invisible.'

'Invisible?' asked the magician.

'Yes,' said the monster.

'Why?' asked the magician.

'Because I am so ugly people run away from me and they can't run away from someone they can't see.'

'All right,' said the magician, 'I will give you the magic, but although it will make you invisible, you could be in for a few surprises.'

The magician put the hat on the table, waved his magic wand, tapped the hat three times and said, 'Abracadabra.'

The monster put the hat on his head, looked in the mirror and saw, nothing. Then he took it off again and saw his reflection. On and he disappeared, off and there he was.

He thanked the magician, put his hat back on his head and walked outside, knowing that no one would be able to see him.

All the way home on the bus, passengers came and went, but no one moved to another seat because they were afraid of him.

Something strange, however, was happening inside his hat. He could feel something soft on the top of his head, like cotton wool. He couldn't wait to get home so he could find out what it was.

As soon as he got back to his cave he took off his magic hat and out fell a string of chiffon scarves all tied together. There were red ones and green ones and yellow ones and orange ones, white ones and pink ones and blue ones. On and on they went until he had enough scarves to hang round his walls like Christmas garlands.

The next day he put on his hat and went for a walk along the high street and while, for once, nobody crossed over to walk on the other side of the road, again, something very strange was happening to the top of his head.

First he felt a scratching, then he felt a fluttering and then he felt something sharp pecking at his forehead. He couldn't wait to get home and take off his magic hat.

As he lifted it off, out flew not one, not two, not three, but a hundred white doves. There were so many feathers flying around his cave he couldn't stop sneezing.

The following day he went out again and, rather nervously put on the hat. No sooner had he set it on his head than he felt something fluffy and tickly inside it, so he cut short his walk and ran home to see what was happening.

This time, nothing fell out of his hat and nothing flew out, but when he looked in his mirror he found he had a rabbit sitting on top of his head. He put the rabbit on the floor, put his hat back on and took it off again. There, on his head, was another rabbit. He put that one on the floor beside the other one. Then he put his hand inside his hat and pulled out another rabbit by its ears. He peered inside and saw nothing, but each time he put his hand in, out came another rabbit.

All night he pulled out rabbits, till there was only enough room on the floor for his monster feet and still the doves kept flying round his cave and still he kept sneezing because of their feathers and still the scarves hung round his walls like garlands.

The next day he didn't wear his hat; he put it in a bag and carried it back to the magician's house.

'Please, please Mr Magician,' he said, 'take away the magic from my hat. My home is full of rabbits and doves and scarves. I don't care if I am so ugly people run away from me. I just want to be myself again.'

The magician looked at the monster and said, 'I will take away the magic. What's more, I will stop people from running away from you.'

He took out his magic wand, walked around the monster muttering strange words, then tapped him on the shoulder three times and said, 'Abracadabra.'

The next time the monster looked in the mirror he was not a monster at all, but a handsome young man.

'This little bit of magic you can keep forever,' said the magician.

The monster, who was now a handsome young man thanked the magician and went home to his cave full of rabbits, doves and scarves feeling very, very happy.

THE SEQUIN
Eltanto

Her tousled, blonde hair spread over the pink, lacy pillow, Amy frowned as she wobbled her milk tooth back and forth with her little finger. It made a funny clicking sound when she pushed it. Amy wondered if she would still be able to eat her favourite food, fish fingers, or even sausages, when it finally left her. She must get it out before she fell asleep or else she might swallow it and choke, she told herself. Anyway, Amy knew that tiny, clean teeth like hers were worth quite a bit to the fairies with the gossamer wings. Her best friend Clare, who sat next to Amy at school, had 'lost' a tooth only last week.

'The tooth fairies make necklaces with them if they're not rotten of course,' she told her, 'and if you put them under your pillow they fly through your window and leave money there, in exchange for the tooth, I got a whole pound for mine,' she had said, beaming a wide smile, whilst fingering the gap it had left behind.

Amy sat up in bed, deep in thought. Clare had told her to remember to leave the window open a little bit, or else the fairies couldn't fly in. First though the tooth must come out. She wondered how many teeth she needed to lose to be able to buy herself that lovely Barbie mansion for her favourite doll.

The thought spurred her on to try a lot harder to remove that tiresome tooth. She knew it might bleed a bit when it came out, and hoped it wouldn't be too much - not enough to need a transfusion, like her mummy needed when she gave birth to her. No, this was just a little tooth, with small roots, aren't they? Amy wasn't sure, this had never happened to her before.

Fear and uncertainty were creeping into Amy's mind. She started to wish her tooth wasn't wobbly. She could live without that extra pound!

The long, dark night stretched ahead, as did the unknown. Amy began to worry about the fairy or fairies flying through her window. She decided to stay awake so that she might see them, and perhaps speak to them.

Thinking about this made Amy remember what else Clare had said: 'You must be asleep, else they won't come in, you're not allowed to see them, it's unlucky!'

Click, click, click. Amy pushed her tiny tooth back and forth, until a dribble of bloodstained saliva ran out of the corner of her mouth.

Tasting the blood, she switched on her bedside lamp, padded across the soft, pink carpet and picked up her vanity mirror and tissues. Her reflection stared back at her in amazement. There it was, hanging loosely by her bottom lip. *Nearly there,* Amy thought to herself as she knelt on the Barbie-pink duvet, staring in disbelief. She knew it was getting late and her mother would be going to bed soon and would probably look in on her.

One last twist should do it, Amy told herself as she pushed her toes back under the duvet. Screwing up here nose and grasping the tooth in the tissue, she took a deep breath and pulled.

The tiny offender was out at last, safe inside the mish-mash of red, bespeckled paper. So relieved and pleased with herself now, the tiny seven-year-old could at last go to sleep. First though, she must wipe the pearly incisor clean and place it under her pillow. So intent was she, that at first she didn't hear the sound of tiny wings rustling, beating faster and faster. However, when she did she became startled, as her light was on - the fairies would go away again if she saw them. With her heart pounding, Amy turned to switch off the light, only to find that the 'fairies' were indeed only moths, drawn to the light. Her anxiety turned to relief, as she lay down her weary head and with heavy eyes was just about to enter the land of Nod when her mother drifted into the room.

'Aren't you asleep yet my little one? It's very late you know.' With that her mother stroked her hair and kissed her on the cheek. 'Better close your window too, before you catch a chill,' she uttered on the way out of the room. The window was pulled to as her mother left. Amy knew then that her tooth would still be there in the morning.

The early rays of the sun streamed through Amy's bedroom window, as her mother drew back the curtains, 'Time to get up darling,' she smiled, adding, 'don't be too long coming downstairs or you'll be late for school.'

Curled up in a little ball, not wanting to move, Amy wished it was Saturday. She decided to stay in bed a few more minutes, snug and warm, and then have one last look at her tooth before the fairies definitely took it that night. Rubbing her eyes, the pair of tiny hands lifted the crumpled pillow. Amy's jaw dropped in amazement, for lying there in place of her tooth, was a shiny pound coin. But what was that glittering close by it? Was it fairy dust? She picked it up, it shone like a rainbow, it looked like a sequin.

Amy thought that this must be a sign left by a certain fairy, maybe the fairy queen! Yet, how did she get in with the window closed? She must have been very tiny indeed to squeeze through any cracks.

With renewed faith, the little girl dressed hurriedly as she couldn't wait to get to school to see her friend Clare. Placing the coin and sequin in her purse, she rushed downstairs and into the kitchen, only to be met by her mother proudly holding up a pair of pure-white wings.

'I've stayed up half the night to finish these for your nativity play Amy, want to try them on? Look, I've even sewn some lovely coloured sequins on them so that they sparkle.

Poor Amy, her dreams had been dashed, tiny fairy indeed. She felt cheated, she was deeply hurt and felt she could never trust her mother again! Oh well, there's still Father Christmas, Amy mused as she stared into her cereal bowl.

Just then, her father, a landscape gardener, breezed through the kitchen, wearing his tatty, old red sweater and carrying a pair of black wellington boots under his arm. Pecking her mother on the cheek, he smiled broadly, ruffled Amy's hair and left for work.

SIR TWEEDYBROW'S QUEST
Doreen Roberts

Princess Felicity was very greedy, always wanting something. New shoes, silk dresses, scrumptious food and beautiful things to decorate her rooms in the palace. The king was unhappy because the princess was spending too much of his money; he must find a husband to feed and clothe her, one that could also supply her with pretty baubles and trinkets to keep her happy. He must find him soon, before she spent all of his money.

The princess did not want a husband, she felt quite content to stay as she was. The greedy Felicity had a plan. She told the king to find a tall, handsome knight in shining armour. They would be married but first he must present to her one gift. A thing to be admired more than herself, it would need to delight her eyes, have a divine fragrance to tickle her nose, most of all it must give her eternal happiness. The gift would need to be small enough to hold in one of her tiny hands.

'I will only marry the knight able to bring me this one simple offering,' she said defiantly.

The king was pleased; he knew lots of handsome knights loved the beautiful, but greedy Princess Felicity, he told them of her request. Alas, they did not love her enough to search for the gift she desired; except for one unfortunate, handsome knight, Sir John Tweedybrow. He made a promise to search the universe for the small treasure to please the princess, on return from his journey he would expect to make her his wife.

Sir John was a fool! He thought the task would be easy. He set off on his quest wearing his Sunday-best armour, with his long, brown hair flowing from beneath his helmet. He sat astride Scrunch, his favourite horse. It carried Sir John into the waiting world. He was sure of swift success.

The greedy Felicity laughed as the handsome knight rode away, she thought the task she had set was impossible and hoped never to see Sir John Tweedybrown again.

Days passed without luck; the days turned into weeks, weeks into months until Sir John realised the gift Princes Felicity desired was not going to be easy to find. He travelled on with hope in his heart and a sore bottom; his armour was very hard. Scrunch the horse was tired and hungry, but the faithful pair journeyed on through villages and towns, mountains and valleys. Months turned into years, the once handsome knight was not so handsome now. His brown hair had turned a grizzled grey to match his tweedy eyebrows. His shining armour had turned rusty, it squeaked at every move. Sir John's bones squeaked with old age, Scrunch could only clip-clop slowly as he carried his foolish master in the never-ending search for the impossible.

One misty morning as Scrunch slowly made his way along a mountain path, his four aching hooves slipped on the crumbling stones. Sir John was thrown down the mountainside; with a clatter of rusty armour he rolled noisily to end with a big crash and a bump on his head. The helmet was so rusty it had broken into pieces. *I must be dying,* he thought as he closed his eyes in sleep.

He was awakened by the buzzing of a large bumblebee sitting on the end of his long, red nose. Gently opening one eye at first, then the other, he found he was lying on a soft bed covered with white linen sheets; a sweet perfumed breeze was blowing through the open window of a tiny room. He felt more peaceful than he had ever been in his whole life. It was the most comfortable bed he had ever slept in; he heard more busy buzzing bees outside the window; he sat up and looked around, to his delight he saw a garden more beautiful than any other he had seen in all his years of travel. The door opposite the bed opened quietly, his nose was tickled by the smell of freshly baked bread. In the doorway stood two quaint figures, a man and a woman, they were smiling, he thought they must be the happiest people in the world.

The plump, old lady held a tray with a plate of newly baked bread and a jug of wine. Percy Popple and his wife Poppy left the food and wine on a small table by the comfortable bed, Poppy Popple invited the old, grey-haired knight to eat, then he must join them downstairs. Sir John Tweedybrow ate the simple food, put on a clean shirt he found hanging behind the door, then ventured down the narrow stairway. Sitting in their bright, cosy kitchen were Percy and Poppy Popple, their table was laden with lovely food.

Percy Popple said, 'Sad old knight, you are welcome to share all we have until you are well enough to continue on your journey; my wife and I found you at the bottom of a mountain and carried you here to rest. We always have plenty of the simple things of life; they arrive as if by magic.'

'Come into the garden,' said Poppy, 'your horse is grazing in the lush grass in the meadow, he is quite content.'

Sir John Tweedybrow walked into the beautiful garden. Close by was Scrunch, he seemed younger, happier and quite frisky, which was strange after such a nasty tumble down the mountain. As Sir John looked around he noticed that every rose was yellow, each the same except for one, it was more beautiful than the others. The garden was full to overflowing with beautiful yellow roses, bees were happily buzzing from bloom to bloom.

'Do you like our rose garden?' asked Percy and Poppy Popple. 'Our one special rose blooms every year; it has just one flower, and in the centre of its tiny petals grow three more tiny buds, they turn into three pretty little roses and are blessed with the most delightful perfume, each one holds a wish. We know this tiny flower is magical, each year we give this special rose to someone in need, hoping it will bring them eternal happiness.'

Sir John's eyebrows twitched up and down as he studied the delicate beauty of the yellow rose, it was the most exquisite flower he had ever seen, more beautiful than Princess Felicity. He must have this rose; it was the simple gift he had searched many years for. He asked Percy and Poppy if he might buy the rose, they refused, telling him it would spoil the magic charm of happiness if exchanged for money, but they would give it him without payment because he looked sad, tired and old. They thought he needed simple beauty and happiness in his life.

Within a few days of comfort and tender care with Percy and Poppy Popple, he put on the remains of his rusty armour, sat astride Scrunch to start the homeward journey. He would present the beautiful Princess Felicity with the rose, he was sure such a treasure would please her. Poppy Popple placed the perfect rose into a tiny basket to keep it safe on the old knight's journey home.

After a few days happily travelling they approached the castle. He noticed it looked neglected and sad, bedraggled weeds hung from its crumbling walls. The princess' old man servant Twurp appeared at the broken door.

'Hello Twurp,' said Sir John, 'I have travelled far to see the Princess Felicity.'

'I am pleased to see you Sir John,' said Twurp, 'I will take you to see the princess. She is greedier and fatter than when you left; after her father died she wasted most of his money on food for herself and forgot everything else.'

Sir John followed Twurp, Princess Felicity's faithful servant; he was old now and limped on bandy legs. As the door to the princess' room opened, the old knight stood aghast, he was horrified and could see no beautiful princess. He was confronted by a large, gruesome, old lady with long, straggling, grey hair. She sat at a table covered with food of all descriptions. Some was mouldy, mice were running in and out of the dirty dishes, the ogre was pushing food into her mouth so fast it was dropping onto her dirty, stained dress. She looked up at Sir John without stopping to rest; she spoke with her mouth full of gingerbread sandwich topped with hot yellow mustard. It showered onto the knight's rusty armour making noisy pings and twangs as it landed.

'So you have returned foolish knight, I hoped you were lost, what do you want old man, tell me quickly then leave!'

'I have returned with the gift you desired,' Sir John replied meekly as he opened the basket holding the rose.

Fat Princess Felicity peered at it, with mustard and gingerbread dribble running down her five fat chins.

'So you think that rose is to be admired more than me do you? I suppose it is small enough to hold in my tiny hand!' She made to grab the precious flower with a hand that had grown fat and knobbly. 'Does it have the exquisite fragrance I wanted?' she screeched. 'I must admit it is pleasing to the eye, but what are those three green buds in its centre, they spoil it. I don't like them, let me pull them out now.'

Sir John Tweedybrow was becoming impatient with the princess; her eyes bulged with greed, he knew he could never make this horror his wife. How could he escape, what could he do?

He said, 'Dear princess, the buds are three wishes for you alone, they are to bring eternal happiness, this is a magical rose so make your wishes quickly and carefully.'

Princess Felicity grabbed the rose once again shouting as she pulled one green bud, 'I wish for more food and drink,' she screamed with laughter as the whole room suddenly filled with scrumptious goodies. 'Ohh, I wish I had more,' she yelled and pulled another bud from the centre of the rose. More food piled high on top of the first lot, her eyes popped with pleasure at the sight of so much food. She had used two of the three wishes.

'I have made a big mistake,' he cried, 'I do not want you for my wife; your greed has turned you into a fat monster. I have been foolish and wasted my life on you.'

The ugly princess stuffed more food into her mouth as she laughed and screamed, crumbs spattered across the table. In anger she pulled the last bud from the rose throwing it at the sad knight.

Stamping her fat foot she yelled without thinking, 'I wish you would stop grumbling and go away Sir John, go back to where you came from and leave me to this lovely food.'

Her third wish was granted; Sir John Tweedybrow found himself back in Percy and Poppy Popple's garden of yellow roses, relieved to be out of the sight of the ugly princess; all was quiet here. It had taken too much of his time trying to make her happy, now he wanted rest with his faithful horse Scrunch. Percy and Poppy Popple welcomed them back; they showed Sir John to a tiny cottage where he could spend the rest of his days thanking the magic rose for giving him the gift of a quiet life, which he deserved.

Poppy said, 'You did your best to make the greedy Princess Felicity happy, now your quest is over. As repayment for the years you wasted on her, the magic rose will bring you eternal happiness and contentment for the rest of your life.'

And so it was.

A GOLDEN LABRADOR NAMED SUZZY
Zoe French

Suzzy didn't start life very well. The people who had her did not love her. She made a mess on their carpet and was banished to the outside shed, which was cold and draughty. They also forgot to feed her so that she lost weight and her coat hung on her bones. She was leading a terrible life and wondered if it was worth living. She didn't think anyone would love her now, she was already seven months old. The people put an advert in the paper to sell her for £120.

I happened to see that advert and phoned after her. The man brought her to us in the evening. She was just skin and bone, lifeless and afraid. I picked her up, she was no weight at all and just hung her head. When I lifted her head her eyes should have been bright with mischief, they were dull as if she had already given up. I was extremely angry, not with Suzzy, but with the people who had had her. I asked the man why she was so thin and lifeless. He said he had to shut her in a shed because she had made a mess on their brand new carpet. I asked him if he knew what newspaper was for. His reply, he couldn't see the carpet with that down. I also asked him why she was so thin and all her bones stuck out. He said when she was in the shed they had forgotten to feed her, then had the cheek to say if we didn't want her he would have her back. I told him over my dead body would he get her back. I told him he had the money he had asked for, now he could go. He said there are no papers with her you know. I told him I didn't need papers, she was a pet not a puppy factory.

The first thing I did was get her to a vet. I carried her in my coat. The vet was as angry as I was. He said she only looked like a two-month-old puppy and was amazed when I told him she was seven months old. I told the vet the whole story, giving the name, address and phone number of the people. He said he didn't hold out much hope for her. He wrote on top of her records that she was an anorexic not expected to live, given seven days. I gathered her up more angry and upset than I had ever been in my life. I was damned if she would die, not if I could help it.

Once we were home I put down several dishes of food. She lay on the carpet, the food untouched. I picked her up and put her on my lap taking up one of the dishes and opening her mouth. I put a small amount of food in her mouth, brushing her throat gently until she swallowed, then another small amount. So this went on until she had eaten about half the dish. At least she had some food in her. She went to sleep on my lap with me stroking her very gently. When she awoke she was still there and put her head up for the first time. Lifting her up I took her outside for her toilet then showed her how to get through the dog flap so that she could come and go into the garden whenever she wanted to.

After that she followed me around wherever I went. I fed her every few hours, usually by hand, but at last she was feeding. I was thrilled and knew she would live now. Then she had severe diarrhoea. I thought I had lost her because nothing the vet did helped her. I was at my wits end. I gave her a tablet that had been advertised on telly for adults. It stopped the diarrhoea dead. I keep the tablets in case it starts up again.

Suzzy went back to the vets a fortnight later for her injections. The vet didn't think it was the same dog, there was such a change in her. She was full of life and mischief just as she should have been all her little life. Suzzy had put on weight and looked fitter.

She is now four years old, very much loved, and in return is a very loving dog who won't let me out of her sight. Needless to say, she is a mummy's girl. Suzzy has a sister called Sally who is a blue merle border collie. They adore each other and as far as mischief goes, what one can't think of the other can.

THE STORY OF MARTHA THE MOUSE
Frances Gibson

Martha Mouse was very proud of her new straw box home. She spent all day determined to have her house spotless, not a straw out of place. With all the excitement of moving furniture and fitting a fluffy white carpet, she forgot to collect some food for her four baby mice, who were already making a terrible noise because they were so hungry.

Off Martha Mouse ran to the cow shed thinking she could collect pickles of grain that had fallen off the feeder wagon, but there at the door was the big cat, Ginger. It was much too dangerous to stop for grain so Martha slipped away very quietly.

Poor Martha was upset. *I'll go across the yard to the chicken house, surely I'll find some left over grain,* she thought, but there at the chicken house door Darkie the Collie lay curled up fast asleep. Darkie slept with one eye open ready to jump if called to collect the sheep. It was much too dangerous. *I'll have to go home,* thought Martha. Suddenly she heard a noise as Granny Huddles' door was opened. Martha thought, *perhaps I'll get plenty of food in Grandma Huddles' house, but if the door closes I won't be able to get out. What would happen to my four hungry mice? No, I can't go in there.*

Martha was tired and upset. She heard someone coming out of Granny Huddles' kitchen. She hid behind the mop bucket watching patiently as little Sarah put down a few broken biscuits and pieces of bread. As Sarah closed the door behind her, Martha scurried off with all the food she could carry to her four hungry babies.

Martha Mouse was glad to have her hungry babies fed. She read them a story and tucked them into a feather bed. Never again did Martha forget to keep a store of food. Exhausted Martha Mouse fell fast asleep.

KING MAVERICK
James Stephen Cameron

As the story goes, long, long, long ago in the kingdom of Sussex in the year 1455 there lived a handsome king named King Maverick. A very lucky man indeed, being born with tremendous wealth, inherited from his family. Aristocrats from birth, with peerage and title, and with a prestigious coat of arms showing two proud bulls, two pheasants and a cock which were crossed with two golden swords upon the wooden decorative plaque, which was placed above the entrance to the great, magnificent hall of Dukesbury Manor. With his great dog named Sebastian, a spotted Dalmatian, the king often liked to poach on his own lands, shooting wild prey and animals with his large wooden crossbow, where his faithful companion would retrieve his master's catch, where he would receive food and warm greetings for his quickness and obedience in the field by the woods and forests.

It was a normal day like any other. The sky was blue with a few white clouds passing overhead and it was spring in the month of April. Wild birds sang merrily, chirping away at this and that. The king went further and further into the green and brown forest hoping to bag plenty of pheasant, badger, rabbit and hare.

After one hour the king had travelled too far than necessary, as he usually did. The forest became dark and eerie with hardly any light penetrating through the tops of the tall trees of oak, ash, elm, silver birch and many others. There was a unusual quietness, almost foreboding as he walked amongst the large green ferns. All the songs of birds and creatures of the woods had mysteriously stopped. A chill went down the king's spine with trepidation, fearing what was to come next, for he had unwittingly lost all sense of direction. Even Sebastian was nervous, whimpering by his master's side on occasion. Would he retrace his steps? But how could he, for he had left no permanent markers, like broken twigs and such like. He looked upwards and everything seemed odd underneath the canopy of trees, as if everything was spinning around and around in a never-ending circle, which made him quite dizzy at times of inspection. All sense of time had completely gone as he walked on hoping for a miracle of sorts, a clearing or landmark which he could navigate from.

Suddenly from the corner of his eye he noticed a quick movement within the vegetation and shrubbery. Small creatures darting, jumping, flying hitherto all about him. The dog was first to notice this oddity and mystery and his hackles rose upon his back like fine pine needles. Instinctively Sebastian let out a long laborious howl at the frightening encounter. King Maverick automatically checked his crossbow and was ready to fire at a moment's notice. The fear was overwhelming, with cold nervous sweat pouring from his face. He wiped his brow fervently stopping underneath a large oak tree, his only immediate protection. Hideous shrieks now permeating the forest gave one the screaming abb-dabbs. What ill-fortune was this that lurked and hid in the woods of Sussex was anybody's guess. His heartbeat laboured and his chest heaved in anticipation.

Suddenly black bats in their thousands appeared, flying madly in a swarm and frenzy. The king knocked a few with his outstretched arms flailing. Complete horror filled his mind as the black mass of flying creatures dissipated away from the area of the forest as quickly as they had come.

Sebastian was injured slightly, with a couple of wounds upon his back which trickled with blood. With new-found strength the brave king walked on slashing with his sword, hoping he could find somewhere safe before nightfall set in. The clever darting creatures were still evident though - dark green and red with shimmering eyes that looked right though one's soul. Frustrated, King Maverick pleaded to the Almighty for salvation from his misery. There had to be a way out from this nightmare, which had only just begun. As he slashed further through the vegetation there was a clearing of grass and rocks where he discovered a caravan likened to a gypsy's, painted in greens, yellows, reds and blue with gold decorative trim and two brown horses tethered alongside, eating grass. As he approached he noticed a sign which read, 'Be brave and know your future. I, Stella the Hag of Kent, the great Queen of Fortune. Do come inside and quiet your mind with destiny and fortune'. And all about came many disturbing goblins whom sat like little monkeys as they fed themselves with nuts and wild red berries, Scratching their pointed noses and talking in some strange dialect that King Maverick did not know. Sebastian barked with terrible whines like that of a wolf at these strange creatures. Were they spirits of the woods and common forest? Did they represent harm and mischief?

Inside the caravan the king heard a woman's voice cackle like an old witch. 'Who is there? Is it a trespasser who comes to rob an old spinster of all she owns?'

'No,' he shouted back, 'I am King Maverick of Sussex, a kind considerate soul whom only wants peace and harmony from his travels.'

'Oh, you had better come inside then stranger, and why you're at it, leave your animal outside. It shall not be harmed in any way,' replied the Hag of Kent wickedly. And up the wooden steps through the curtains King Maverick climbed to await his future fate. 'As I have expected and foretold, you come unto this world with brave intentions. Please be seated and calm your nerves.'

The king quickly looked about at her quarters, where an old spinning wheel was being worked by the witch of Kent. By her side was a small, round table and upon it was a black cloth with something hidden underneath. Around her head was a red and black silk scarf knotted at the side. She smiled at her quest, showing black teeth, her pointed chin full of horrible warts, with a protruding bent nose to match her ugly appearance.

'Oh do be seated King Maverick, there at the opposite end of the table.' The witch brought out what looked like a gold framed triangle shaped pyramid and underneath its centre hung a pendulum with a crystal at its end. 'Oh, the future, the future. You do have a future don't you King Maverick?' declared boldly the cunning witch.

He sat down apprehensively thinking of what all this meant. After all, he had only gone for a stroll to catch wild flying birds and wood animals, an innocent past-time that he often took. Then the witch asked the king to blow upon the hanging pendulum which began to swing in a clockwise direction, around and around it went, slowly then faster and faster.

'Oh I see a princess, one that will become your queen. But there is great danger and peril to overcome first, might I add.

He dared to ask more of her inquisitions. 'And what is the danger, old woman, that you see with your third eye?'

'Now that you ask, I must consult the crystal ball first, and scry accordingly, and see what takes shape before I can tell you.' She smiled and removed the black cloth from her large glass ball. After some seconds, first a milky cloud appeared within the prism of glass, and then another. 'Oh it is synonymously obvious and portentous with ill omens of doom. Only the immortal gods can save you. I shall try my last divination rites outside young man. So follow me.'

Reluctantly the brave king did as she wished of him. To the right-hand side of the caravan was a large black cauldron which was standing above a lit fire. He watched fascinated as she threw in dead toads, frogs, newts, spiders etc.

Chanting wildly the hag went about her business, walking around and around, whilst placing inside her crooked wooden stick, moving all the dead creatures within the boiling waters for some considerable time. 'There is a beast that hides within this very forest, with eyes of a black wolf. It watches you, even now, it knows your soul King Maverick. You must be audacious if you wish to survive. The beast will devour you if you do not succeed with your mission.'

'But how is this? What mission do you talk about old woman of the forest?' questioned the brave king anxiously.

'There are three women who wait your return. One will become your queen, but which one? Only one is genuine, and the other two are fearful creatures of the night, one whom is jealous and one whom is dangerous beyond all imagination. Only one is pure and righteous . . . and a word of warning, one of them has the power to turn you into dust, no longer of this Earth . . . and remember, you will need a mirror to unfathom this mystery. A mission of temptation and pitfalls. No man is immune from the secret worlds that we live in. You must be gone now and find your way back through the dark forest tomorrow,' challenged the hag.

After a worrying night the brave king awoke, had breakfast and stole away from the witch's caravan, just himself and his faithful dog, where they both journeyed back into the forest to face the fears of the unknown. With audacious strength and commitment King Maverick swore allegiance to the cause, with new-found courage about his demeanour, whilst hacking down vegetation and wild tall brambles, thorns and bushes. But the eyes of the forest were watching his every movement and behold when he was in the middle of the forest, a large lizard creature blocked his path to freedom, spitting all fire and poison in his direction, hell bent on devouring him. Sebastian fought by his master's side with heroism and untold courage, whilst King Maverick fired his crossbow, hitting the ferocious beast through its darkened heart. Two more arrows were needed to finish off the terrible beast of the underworld, where he completed his victory by slaying the dark animal with his golden sword. At last he had championed against the fear within his heart. With new enthusiasm he marched confidently through the remainder of the forest, back to his home, Dukesbury Manor, the victor of this nightmarish challenge.

Three days were to pass when three ladies came on visit by royal carriage from London, all pretenders, and claimants, all wishing to be his queen. The witch's predictions soon came back, haunting the king's mind and heart. How was he to choose correctly which claimant was the real one? He bade them to all come into the great hall of Dukesbury Manor House and make their presence known unto him. The king's manservant soon ushered the three beautiful women in where each made their claims of contest.

The first one, whom was an auburn beauty, declared her rightful heir with manners and etiquette expected from a lady in waiting. The second was a fair blonde lady with ringlets flowing down her alabaster face. And lastly was a red haired beauty whom bowed graciously before his Majesty. Through their mannerisms they all seemed like perfect specimens to court a king as he, but which were the two false ones was the thing in question? The king had an idea, for the truth must be known in affairs of the heart. He purposely upset one maiden with a false accusation. 'Do you come for money alone, and to steal my crown?' he asked the dark haired lady. She fell for his slight trick of conversation, trying hard to defend her position with many answers which were unsuitable. Next he laid out three cards from a pack of 52. One was the 10 of spades, one was the ace of spades and the third was a queen of hearts. All cards were placed upside down so as not to be seen, then he mixed them around and around, swapping them at leisure. He then asked them to choose separately which card they had picked. Only one lady picked correctly out of the three suits, but the king kept this to himself for a while. He had one remaining trick up his sleeve. Igneous as it was, he remembered the witch's prophesy - a mirror. King Maverick now ordered his personal guard to bring into the room a large gold framed mirror which was quickly brought to him. He quickly noticed two of the women who suddenly became quite nervous and on edge with themselves at this simple request. King Maverick smiled inwardly knowingly that he had caught the two impostors out when he dared them to look at themselves for one minute in duration. Only one woman seemed confident as she walked forward and gazed at her own reflection - the lady whom picked the queen of hearts from the shuffled playing deck.

'I am waiting,' said the king.

The two other women fought with themselves at such a command. For there was no true reflection from the other two women, none at all. They both turned to dust as each one gazed upon the other. And the queen of hearts stepped forward, the lady with blonde ringlets, the real lady in waiting.

Eventually they were both married in a beautiful wedding ceremony which lasted two whole days. King Maverick had won his lady at last, simply by shuffling the deck of cards.

SARAH, HER FRIENDS AND THE LEPRECHAUN
D M Burnett

Sarah and her two friends, Laura and Elizabeth, chased out of the school yard running full pelt, the school left behind and soon forgotten. They raced down the leafy lane to the farm below nestling at the bottom of the long lane. Sarah lived there with her mother, father and two brothers. Laura and Elizabeth lived close by in the farm cottage - their fathers working for Sarah's father on the farm.

It was early September and very hot. The girls arrived at the farm puffing and blowing, laughing and chiding each other.

'What shall we do?' said Laura.

'I know,' said Elizabeth, 'let's go up the fields. I love the fields, I love the fields,' she chanted. 'Let's go to the pond.'

They made for the five barred gate which led to the fields. Not bothering to open the gate, they climbed over and ran into the fields beyond.

They walked up two grass fields and then turned left for the corn field. The corn had just been harvested and the stubble that was left was short and spiky and difficult to walk on, especially as they had already discarded their shoes and stockings. They soon decided to put them back on again and then raced along the grass verge bordering the field.

'I'll . . . I'll have a race with you,' laughed Sarah. 'The first one to the pond gets a present.'

The three of them chased off at break neck speed. Sarah was very fast and left the other two well behind. She threw herself flat down on the grass throwing her arms above her head. 'Hooray, I win. I get a present.'

'Well, you were going to give the present,' said Laura laughingly, 'you can't give yourself the present. What is it anyway?'

Sarah looked sheepishly. 'I don't know yet,' she said, 'I will have to think about it,' and gave the question no more thought.

The pond was their special place. Someone had hung a long rope from one of the branches that stretched across the pond and had tied a loop in the bottom of the rope. They stood on the bank, put one foot in the loop, and swung across landing on the opposite bank. They then pushed off again swinging back and forth, back and forth. Each of them having a turn one after the other until all three of them were so exhausted they lay on the bank looking into the sky and breaking pieces of straw stubble from the earth which they sucked, chewed and then spat out.

They lay there for some time looking up into the sky and into the tree and then suddenly Sarah said in a whisper, 'Can you see anything, up there in the tree? There's a little green man up there amongst the leaves. He's covered with branches and he's lying up there with an umbrella over his head.'

'Oh don't talk such rubbish,' said Elizabeth, 'I can't see anything. Can you Laura?' The question remained unanswered as Laura was far too busy peering into the tree.

The three of them were now glued to the tree and watching for the slightest movement.

Suddenly, as they watched, there was a rustle of leaves before they parted and a light tinkling voice said, 'Hello there you three girls, are you enjoying yourselves? Are you training to be acrobats or something? Why are you so quiet now? I'm real enough you know.'

The three girls jumped up in fright and scampered off as fast as their feet would carry them back to the farm gate, puffing and gasping for breath.

'What shall we do now?' they asked, after getting back their breath.

'Nobody is going to believe us anyway, let's keep it a secret and tell no one. Tomorrow night we'll go to the pond again and see if he's there. We'll meet tomorrow, 4 o'clock after school at the farm gate.'

Sure enough at 4 o'clock the next afternoon the three friends met as arranged. They chatted and laughed about the happenings of the day at school, but really there was only one thought on their minds, to get up the fields as quickly as possible and find out if their imaginations had been playing tricks on them.

They walked briskly up the fields. When they got near to the particular field where the swing was their steps started to slow down and they walked apprehensively wondering if they should go any further, but gradually they made their way to the pond again and the swing. They sat on the bank of the pond pensively giving an occasional furtive glance up into the tree and wondering if they dare look.

Eventually they heard a rustling in the leaves and they parted again, then they heard the voice. 'Hello there my beauties, have you come to see me again? Did you wonder if I was real yesterday? I'm real enough you know. I'm a leprechaun - I live here. I won't hurt you. I've seen you several times before but you haven't seen me. Now, shall I tell you a story?'

The three girls looked at each other and didn't know what to say.

'Well no,' said Laura, 'we . . . we can't stay. We have to get back home don't we Sarah, don't we Elizabeth?'

'Oh yes,' said the two girls in unison, 'we can't stay.'

'Will you be back tomorrow then?'

'Well maybe, maybe,' answered Sarah.

And so the three girls returned to the farm not daring to have any more conversation with the little man. A little afraid and wondering whether to forget the whole thing, or go and see him again.

Back at the farm gate Sarah saw her brother James and decided to let him in on the secret. She then regretted it because he burst out laughing, and laughed and laughed until the three girls were really embarrassed.

'Oh what silly little things you are,' he said, 'there aren't any such things as leprechauns. Wait until I tell the others, they won't half laugh. They'll think you are proper silly.'

'Alright,' said Laura, 'if that's the way you feel about it we won't tell you anymore. But if you don't believe us the next time we go you come with us, then you'll see for yourself.'

'Tomorrow then, shall we all meet tomorrow?' asked Sarah.

'Alright,' said James, 'I'll be there.'

The next night they all turned up at the farm gate as arranged, but to their dismay James was not on his own, with him were his three friends, that made four boys and three girls.

'Good heavens!' said Laura, 'we shan't see any leprechauns, you'll all frighten him off.'

The boys raced off ahead of the girls, singing and shouting and making a right hullabaloo. The cows, wondering what was happening, fled in all directions frightened by the noise they were making. The girls chased after the boys and started to have a rough and tumble - knocking each other about and pushing each other over - until they all fell laughing and squealing on the ground, and then kicking and fighting each other.

'Oh goodness,' said Laura, 'if we carry on like this that little leprechaun will hide himself forever. Let's go and see if we can find him.'

They walked down the field where he was and when they got nearer to the swing and the tree where he lived, they heard a noise. It sounded like a penny whistle being played. They all stood still and listened and then walked timidly towards the tree and there in the middle of the pond sat the little green man on a large toadstool playing a whistle.

'Hello there, have you come to see me again? How lovely, and brought your friends as well. Goodness me, I am honoured today. Now what is all this then? Have you come out of curiosity, or perhaps you have just come to see me?'

'Well,' said Sarah, 'my brother didn't believe me when we said we had seen a leprechaun so we said come with us and we will prove it!'

'So now . . . so now, what about it James and you lot that have tagged along, do you see anything or are we seeing things?'

'Oh no,' said James, 'we can see him all right. We have never seen one before, and he speaks as well. I think we had better leave him to his play.'

'Well now my lads, are you going to leave me and so soon? That's a nice thing to do when you have come all this way to see me. Aren't you going to stop and have a word with me? Tell me what you have been doing today.'

'Well no, you would not be interested, at least I don't think you would,' said James, suddenly blushing remembering what he had been up to that day at school.

'Oh well, just as you like then, go and leave me and see if I care!' said the little leprechaun.

The children made their way back home again, now almost silent and seemingly lost for words.

'What do you make of him then?' asked James. 'We can't tell anyone, they won't believe us, just think we have all gone mad. I think we ought to say nothing and keep our mouths shut.'

They all agreed.

Several weeks later the children had all gathered again at the farm gate.

Elizabeth suddenly said, 'How about the little man, shall we go and see if he is there up in the tree?'

They all looked at each other impishly. Then suddenly they took off, not waiting for an answer. They jumped the gate and belted up the fields as fast as their legs could carry them.

They soon reached the pond and the swing. They played around, swinging across the pond on the rope, back and forth, back and forth, squabbling whose turn it was next. Eventually exhausted, they all flopped on the ground.

They were now all quiet and started to peer into the tree.

Suddenly, without warning, a voice said, 'Oh hello, hello, you have come back at last. I'm so pleased, I thought you had forsaken me and I'm so lonely. All my friends have gone and I'm left here all alone. Will you do me a favour?'

'What sort of favour?' asked James. 'We don't say we will do any favours until you tell us what you want.'

'Well, you know that spinney over there? I think I have some friends and relations over there. Do you think you could possibly take me there, in your pocket.'

'I suppose we could,' replied James. 'But what do we get for all our trouble?'

'Oh you children, you are all the same. You won't do anything for nothing. Don't you ever think of doing anything just to please anybody? And without wanting anything in return? Well anyway, if you take me there I will think about giving you a present, or maybe a surprise.'

'Oh alright then,' said James, 'hop into my pocket and we'll take you over there.'

So the children, all seven of them, trooped across the ploughed field. Their shoes were covered with sludge. It had been raining heavily and they were filthy. The mud was up to their knees as they splished and splashed in the sludge.

'I hope this is going to be worth it,' moaned James. 'Look at the state we are in. We won't half get into trouble when we get back home. Where do you want putting when we get there and how do we find your friends?' he asked of the leprechaun.

'Well,' he answered, 'you just enter the wood and I will show you where to go. You just go along a certain bluebell path and when you reach a circle of trees I will be able to tell you which one to stop at. Put me on your shoulder and I'll guide you there.'

And without more ado the little man sprang out of James's pocket onto his shoulder.

On entering the wood James slipped, lost his footing, and fell headlong into a bed of nettles. The little man lost his balance and fell with a splash into a ditch filled with water.

'Get me out, get me out,' he yelled in his high pitched voice. 'I'm drowning, drowning,' he cried.

All the children rushed to his aid, except James. He was dancing around with pain for he had been badly stung all over with the nettles. 'Find me a dock leaf one of you, quickly, I'm in agony,' he yelled.

Laura found one easily enough and dabbed the stings with it.

'Give it here, give it to me,' he shouted, grabbing the leaf, 'and find me another.'

'Manners, manners, where've your manners gone?' asked Laura.

'Sorry, sorry,' said James, 'but these stings are driving me mad.'

'Well come on now then,' said the leprechaun, 'let's find my friends.' He had soon recovered from his soaking and had now jumped onto Laura's shoulder. She felt a bit uncomfortable having a leprechaun perched on her shoulder.

Eventually they all started trekking off again through the wood. The little man out in front on Laura's shoulder followed by James and his three friends, and Sarah and Elizabeth bringing up the rear.

The leprechaun suddenly let out a shriek in his high pitched voice, 'There, there, look my friends and relations.' He took one leap from Laura's shoulder and scuttled into the undergrowth.

'Where's he gone?' shouted James. 'Where's he gone? Can you see him?'

Then, quite suddenly, they saw him in the midst of a small ring of these little men. They were all sitting on toadstools and puffing away on little clay pipes. In fact, to all intents and purposes, the children seemed to have been forgotten completely. And they were so mesmerised with what they were seeing, they had all flopped to the ground and were engrossed in watching the small men. Actually, they had never ever been so quiet.

Sarah said in a whisper, 'Who's going to believe us? Nobody will believe that in the middle of this spinney is a place like this where leprechauns live. Everyone will think we are making it up, or gone crackers.'

Quite suddenly their little leprechaun turned to his friends and said, 'Look, look, these are my friends. They have brought me across from yonder tree. Aren't they good, aren't they sweet?'

James squirmed, he didn't like it one bit being called 'sweet'.

The little man went on, 'I think for their reward we will let them see us always whenever they come into the spinney. But only when they come without more friends. If they bring anyone else to our secret place, we will be invisible.'

'Yes, yes, very much so,' said the others. 'We shall be visible only to these special ones.'

Shortly afterwards they said goodbye to their new-found friends. Their own little leprechaun ran after them. 'Remember now,' he said, 'come on your own, if you don't you won't see us.'

'We'll remember,' they all shouted, turning and waving before running back to the farm.

They were all very happy and smiling for they had a secret and they would tell no one. And after all they had seen the leprechauns because they were special, the leprechauns had said so.

And wouldn't you like to know what happened next? I bet you would.

CAPTAIN BOBBITT AND THE CURSE OF
THE CRYSTAL EYE
Glenwyn Evans

Part 2 - Broken

Captain William Kidd Bobbitt was the guardian of the Golden Secret (a golden locket that hung round his neck), a secret that only a few knew. One was Lady Byrd Bird, whom whilst on a fly about mission one day mysteriously vanished . . .

Dungbeetle's work, no doubt (some would argue). How right they were, for Lord Ruthless Dungbeetle and his sage and onion fiend-friend, Evm Lizard Wizard, had seized the golden locket, leaving Bobbitt in the vicious claws of the Bug'nator . . .

'It's your end!' snarled the Bug'nator, grinding his sharp needle-like teeth, his vile, sickening, hot breath suffocating the captain, slowly.

'No!' gasped he, deliriously, 'I have to escape.'

Tears streaming his little pink face, Bobbitt lashed out fiercely, wriggling, kicking; the Bug'nator's claws ripped through to his flesh, the fresh blood tingled excitement.

Suddenly two pistol shots splintered the ceiling above the Bug'nator's head. Sharpishly the creature turned, towering to its full height, hovering the five flea-at-arms, who, for a moment, stood mortified.

Crack! Crack! Two more shots whistled the air.

Pieces of debris hit the Bug'nator's head; it screamed and shrieked angrily. Jon Chan-lee rushed up, in a flying feet-first dive he kicked his chin.

The Bug'nator dropped the captain and in screaming terror grabbed the Crystal Eye, and smashed through a plate glass window, taking with it the golden locket.

'All is lost,' admitted Bobbitt dolefully after he had recovered all his strength a few days later. 'Lads, I have lost the golden locket, and who knows what will become of us . . . '

'Yer listen ta me,' growled Rapper-der-Flea, 'Bossy Bob-bob-bitt, why we five, who saved yer life, will search dis islan' f'r der Crystal Eye, and if you lead der way, Bossy Bob-bob-bitt, we get back tha' golden locket!'

The crew cheered.

Bobbitt, overwhelmed, paced the poopdeck with a peculiar hop and sprightly little bounce. He'd turn, scratch beneath the patch covering his bad eye and gaze, despairingly.

A solitary tear formed upon an ashen face from his one good eye; lips trembling a little, with grave concern, reluctantly he said, 'True, the curse of the Crystal Eye must be broken . . . ' and so declared the untold truth, that of which he'd learned from the Lady of the Locket, the ill-wind that sighs the golden land of El Bug-rado . . . and of the pure evil created - the Bug'nator. Had it not in a short space of time, already devoured and slayed the inhabitants of this fair land?

And all the crew from bosun Sammy to the least Mr Yen Tong (peg-leg, the one the captain saved from drowning), in one joyous voice cried their 'yeahs'.

Bobbitt, abashed, bit his bottom lip. 'You have all spoken well and I am deeply touched. Out of all of you only these five I must choose . . . '

The five he picked were Ercufleas, Rapper der Flea, Tiny 'Foghorn' Flea, Yoo Yoo Flea and last of the fleas, but not the least, Jon Chan-lee Flea.

The day was leaden cast, mucky and humid, a horrid feeling gnawed the five as they sat round the camp fire, roasting marshmallows, listening to Tiny, griping . . .

Bobbitt sprang up, drawing quick his sword. He ushered them to silence. 'Who goes? Friend or foe?' he yelled, but the others who had heard nothing, convinced him he was hearing things.

'Sit Cap'n,' beckoned Yoo Yoo. 'It's just the wind whinnying.'

'Wind, Yoo Yoo?' replied the captain. 'Is not the air still?' He had no sooner finished his sentence when the intruder suddenly burst forth.

Bobbitt's blade flashed, but the creature was very fast and jumped over the sword.

'Who be you?' grunted the varlet, behind a grim, dark mask as cold steel clashed against cold steel.

'Captain William Kidd Bobbitt, and these, my five companions,' with each murderous thrust. 'And you?'

The stranger, frightened and strained, screeched quarter, catching his breath. He drew away and to the others astonishment cried aloud, 'Captain Bobbitt! At last I'm all but saved!'

Bobbitt stood back in wonderment. 'Whom do we address, good sir?' looking at his companions, shrugging.

'I am Robber T de Fly,' bowing courteously, then collapsing into a weary mumbling state. De Fly told them of how he'd had one wing ripped off while trying to escape the evil clutches of Dungbeetle . . . 'and that,' he concluded, 'is how I came to be here, and live the life of a common robber fly, behind the mask of grim . . . '

Bobbitt, being happy with his explanation, in turn, while eating roasted marshmallows, told him of their uncanny quest (but of the locket he said nought).

'You are brave Cap'n and, if you want, I will lead you there, for this island falls foul of nasty tricks.'

Nasty tricks? thought Tiny Flea, suspiciously. Something just did not ring true about this new guy . . .

'Good,' laughed Bobbitt, 'for I have heard fortune favours the brave.'

De Fly laughed coarsely. 'True,' he replied, adding under his breath, 'but it's hunting for the fortune that gets the brave fool killed.'

Under de Fly's guidance, they crept deeper and deeper into the heart of the island, where the stench of death sickened their guts. At first they moved quite briskly, but soon, as day progressed from grey to black, they slowed down.

Now it was pitch-black and Bobbitt called them together, ordering the lifeline to be tied about them.

'Don't worry so Cap'n,' reassured de Fly cheerily, 'no one lives here. The island was deserted, ages ago.'

Tiny jumped on his case, alone, he confronted de Fly. 'Impostor! How can you rob-alivin', when there's no livin' to rob?'

But straightaway de Fly chanted something, and Tiny shrivelled away.

In vain hope one followed the other's footsteps, stumbling and falling, and now to make things worse, they were suddenly engulfed by a thick, gooey spiralling fog.

Yoo Yoo cried out as he fell into quick bog, dragging the others back and, if it hadn't been for the strength of Ercufleas, all the group would have been lost, there and then.

'Where now?' gasped Bobbit. De Fly nodded. 'That old, rickety bridge?'

'Yes . . .' said De Fly, gruffly.

'Is it safe?' enquired Bobbitt. De Fly, shrugged.

'I will go, Capt'n,' insisted Yoo Yoo, Ercufleas, following. The bridge, swayed. A light wind shrilled above their heads, and below, the torrents raged.

'Safe, Cap'n!' cried Yoo Yoo, and just as Bobbitt was about to give the order to cross, the wind whipped up a mighty frenzy; shaking the bridge, it was ripped asunder, and Yoo Yoo and Ercuflea's, were lost.

De Fly, glowered. 'Well, they needed a bath . . . and, the quest, must go on, eh, Cap'n?'

Bobbitt was to shocked to say anything, 'Is there another way?'

De Fly smirked, 'Always . . . another way . . .'

After a long and weary march, which took them some distance up river, they crossed, safely.

'An enchanted gateway,' pointed out De Fly, tactfully.

'Where too?' asked Chan-Lee.

'Elfin-mount.'

'Elfin-mount?' quizzed Bobbitt. 'H-how?'

'Read the words etched into that ugly elm.'

'Hey mon-n,' said Rapper Flea, suspiciously, 'why ain't you?'

De Fly, half laughed, 'Cos man, I can't read.'

Bobbitt, pressed forward, but Chan-Lee acting quickly, forbade him, whispering in his ear: 'Cap'n,' he said, 'Rapper and I will read the words, as of you, be vigilant. For I suspect a trap. Have you not noticed, Cap'n, that the foghorn mouth of Tiny Flea, has been mysteriously, silenced?'

'My goodness,' muttered Bobbitt. He hadn't even noticed!

'Read aloud,' insisted De Fly, derisively.

'Whomso read dis curse aloud, will disappear before the crowd . . .'

At that, they vanished! But, before Bobbitt could utter a word, De Fly, took off.

Sensing betrayal, Bobbitt, drew his sword; the ground, crumbled; trees, were torn up, and sent skudding, like well aimed missiles.

The captain weaved and dived, but then, just when he needed that short respite, the gate peeled back, and a massive creature came hurtling towards him.

The snake-lizard, rearing its diamond shape head, struck savagely; Bobbitt, quick wittedly, counterattacked the blow, slicing one off its deadly, poisonous fangs.

The creature, shocked, recoiled; licking the air with its forked tongue, it tasted Bobbitt's fear; yellow eyes, fiery and bright, its broken fang, regenerated, it struck again.

Bobbitt, bounced, flea metres high into the sky . . .

The creature screeched and hissed; two huge, bat-like wings, hastily wafted the air, revealing two vicious, razor-sharp talons, as it, too, thundered away, after its prey.

As it soared up, Bobbitt, plummeted down.

The creature struck twice in quick succession, then, in a painful hissing gulp, and bloodcurdling shriek, its mouth, foaming a horrid goo, with a mighty crash, it fell to earth, dead.

'Silly creature,' mumbled Bobbitt, 'biting your own tongue!'

Under a sky that seared anger, Bobbitt cautiously, approached Elfinmount; from its topmost peak, skywards bound, a strange, radiant splendour emitted a dazzling display of red and orange hues, flashing, ominously, while the air, thick and clammy, became almost unbreathable, for there, upon its highest pivot, beamed, the Crystal Eye.

The climb was arduous, and wearisome. Thirst, ravaged, clawed his throat; hunger knotted his stomach; every muscle ached and groaned . . . but climb, he must . . .

Each foothold, trembled under his weight; his tiny mitts, clammy, would slip from the mouth of the hole it found. Tired and exhausted, he took rest, panting, breathlessly . . .

Keep going he urged. The quest, it's nearly over!

Gritting, teeth, wiping away dirty sweat, Bobbitt, stretched out; groaning, straining; unexpectedly, he reached and touched the Crystal Eye.

It quivered, weepily; a voice tingled like a myriad triangles, chiming all at once? Slightly, he hesitated . . . determinedly, fearlessly, Bobbitt, growled, snatching it up!

The Crystal Eye screeched, as if startled, exploding with painful delight . . .

Captain Bobbitt, dropped the Eye! He didn't mean too . . . it slipped!

Down, down, down, it fell, exploding into millions of spark-blue flashes, shimmering, glistening, dazzling, glittering, like falling stars.

Into smithereens it blew, like a sharp wind; a refreshing sharp wind; what was once black and decaying, now sparkled life. Elfin-mount, shook and shuddered. Rocks and trees, released its prisoners; the dark veil, lifted, greeting a new warm, glittering dawn.

A bright red sun, blossomed crystal clear skies, like a sun-kissed peach; streams that were once bitter, once more tasted as they should, more refreshing than dew itself, and better still, honey-sweet; tree upon tree, rustled, splendid foliage; from every flower that sprung forth, from where the glittering rainbow hues sparkled, pretty fairies danced, and played music bright, with harps of gold and flutes of silver; a delicious melody, 'Dance of the Dewdrop Queen' . . .

What's more, even Elfin-mount changed. No more did it loom like a giant shark's dorsil fin, but, instead, shook and shimmered, delightfully . . .

A wonderful palace of crimson red; of white sugar pedastels, crowning a beauteous head; of amber nectar, pure and gold; a radiant splendour of treasure and glory, ne'er told. And all this, before the captain's eye, did unfold . . .

'The curse of the Crystal Eye, is broken,' murmured the prisoner of the Crystal Eye, as she brought him down to Earth, to be reunited with his five companions; and that's when he beheld her true glory.

Queen of the Dewdrops, glittering in clustered splendour. And as he bowed, warmly, she said: 'Welcome unto me, Errol Flea,' and Bobbitt, flashing a wide grin, recognised the voice of Lady Byrd Bird. And for a while, everyone was delighted . . .

'Well folks,' rang Rapper, 'dat's where der tale must end, but we'll be back soon, on tha', yer can depend . . .'

Epilogue

'Evm!' growled Dungbeetle, angrily, mitt-fist banging the table. 'For all your black enchantments, worth, I've lost everything! Bobbitt's partying all winter, alive! And that beast you conjured up, the Bug'nator, stole me locket!' He started to cry. 'Now I'll never be worshipped!'

'Sire,' 'hispered Evm, his hot onion breath, shrivelling candles to their wick's-end, 'I 'ave this fantastic, cunning plan . . .'

And Dungbeetle, screamed . . . melting the Forbidden Midden, to a liquid poohy slush.

A FRIEND IN NEED
Molly M Hamilton

Maurice James Mouse was a fine upstanding citizen. He was a helpful and thoughtful neighbour, gave generously to all good causes. His loving wife Mabel, who could never do enough to see that he was always comfortable and happy, adored him. His four daughters, Rosie, Pansy, Daisy and Lily thought that he was the perfect father. To his three sons Melvin, Hector and Joseph he was their strong and fearless hero. In fact I would say you would have to go a long way to find a happier and more loving family.

Their home was warm and cosy, Mabel worked hard to keep it sparkling clean and neat, with all the children having their own jobs to do. It was situated in a corner of the basement of a large old country house. The owners were Lord and Lady Huntsford an old English family. Their ancestors had lived there for many generations. They had three children, Billy (Lord William), Ellen and baby Mary aged two years. Billy and Ellen were twins aged eight years. They were all very spoilt and were allowed to run wild around the house, often eating cakes or biscuits; so there were always crumbs dropped on the carpets. This was very fortunate for Maurice and his family.

I have already mentioned that Maurice was a much loved and highly respected husband, father and member of the community. However Maurice had a deep dark secret, which he had never revealed to a living soul. Maurice had a dreaded fear of *spiders*. The very thought of them would turn him cold. So you can well understand how humiliating it would have been for him if this fact were to be known. Also it would have brought great shame on all the family, when you know that mice are naturally unafraid of spiders.

It was the habit of Maurice and his little family, every Sunday after lunch to take a walk around the large house. They would leave their home in the basement and take a stroll up past the bedrooms and the nursery, along the wide corridors and return down the backstairs home.

Only this Sunday was going to change Maurice's life in a most unexpected and dramatic way that he would never have dreamed of in his wildest dreams.

Now there was an unwritten law among the mice community that under no circumstances would anyone enter into the large living room. There were two very good reasons for this. The first being that Lady

Huntsford was often entertaining her many friends and two (much more important) often lying on the settee, taking up most of it was a large ginger cat.

It is a well known fact that the greatest threat to mice is the *cat*, and this car was (dare I say it?) a very good micer! Many a poor, sad mother could tell you (shedding many tears at the memory) of how she had lost a dear son or daughter by the great teeth or claws of that monster cat.

Returning to Maurice and his family on their Sunday stroll, their youngest son Joseph aged seven was a very high spirited young mouse. This Sunday he was deep in thought as he dawdled behind the rest of his family. He was thinking of how he had boasted to his best friend only last week that he was afraid of nothing. His friend had said, 'I bet you would never go into the living room.'

Joseph hadn't answered. Perhaps that would be going too far. However, the more he thought about it the more excited he became. That would indeed be something to boast about to all his friends, how they would look up to him, he would be a hero. As all this was passing through Joseph's mind they were walking towards the closed door of the living room. Before Joseph realised what he was doing he had left his family and was squeezing himself under the door. With his mind in a daze and his heart hammering loudly against his side, he stood stock still and looked around him.

There was no sign of *the cat!* Gaining confidence somewhat, he started to walk slowly around the large room, keeping close to the skirting board. Wide-eyed and open mouthed he gazed up at the high ceiling, carved with flowers and trailing ferns. His eyes taking in the heavy antique oak furniture that shone in the afternoon sun that streamed through the large bay windows, making the cut glass fruit bowls and vases sparkle on the large carved sideboard. Joseph was admiringly taking it all in and thinking to himself, *gosh! What a lot I will have to tell my friends and how they will envy me.* Just at that moment Joseph felt a cold draught. Someone had opened the door and let the *cat* in!

Joseph half turned to see the large tabby standing not more than a foot from him. His eyes, yellow and gleaming wickedly at Joseph, his mouth half open revealing large sharp teeth. For what seemed ages they stood looking at each other. Joseph unable to move. Then as the cat crouched ready to spring - Joseph found the use of his legs and ran with all his might under the great sideboard pressing himself hard against the wall.

It was some time later before Joseph was missed. Panic broke out.

'Surely he wouldn't have dared to go into the living room,' his mother cried.

'Oh! wouldn't he,' declared Hector, 'only the other day I heard someone bet Joseph he wouldn't dare go in that room and you know what he is like when he has been given a dare.'

His mother knew only too well what her son was like. The thoughts of this brought Mabel to the point of collapse. The girls flocked round their mother in tears.

Maurice, trying hard to stem his own fears forced himself to speak calmly. 'There, don't worry. The cat is mostly in the garden and anyway we are not sure that Joseph has gone into the living room.' He patted his wife's arm, 'just to please you I will go and have a look around the living room door.'

Mabel clung to her husband's sleeve. 'Oh Maurice do be careful,' she sobbed.

'I will be alright,' he said with great confidence that he did not feel. 'You and the children stay here and keep very quiet.' Giving his wife a smile, which he hoped, would reassure her, he crept slowly and silently towards the living room door. Cautiously peering round the open door, his worse fears were realised. Laying full length on the thick red carpet in front of the sideboard was the huge ginger devil himself! His long furry tail was swishing from side to side. Maurice could just make out his small son huddled against the wall at the far back of the sideboard. Despair filled poor Maurice's heart. Whatever could be done to save Joseph? It seemed so hopeless. Perhaps the cat would get tired of waiting and leave, but that was most unlikely. He was very patient when a tasty mouse was in the offering. Night came and early morning dawned. Maurice, keeping his voice hopeful had told his family, much earlier to go home. I am sure I will think of a way to rescue Joseph.

The sun was rising and still the cat showed no sign of leaving his post. It looked like he was getting sleepy, and hope spurred in Maurice's heart. Perhaps he will fall asleep, he thought, then Joseph will be able to escape. It was not to be. The cat did shut one eye and then the other very briefly, licking his red tongue round his mouth. Once Maurice (his heart almost stopping) saw the tabby crawl a shade closer to the sideboard. Joseph was near to collapse. He was cold, hungry and very frightened.

His father feeling increasingly hopeless and so helpless suddenly saw something big and black out of the corner of his eye. It was slowly descending down the wall. Maurice, to his horror realised it was a large spider. He felt he was fainting away, he hung onto the door post. His legs felt like jelly and he felt unable to breathe.

'Please do not be afraid,' the voice that came from the spider was deep and soft and strangely reassuring. 'My friends and I have come to save you.' The spider's voice and his words had a calming effect on Maurice. The spider spoke again. 'We have no desire to harm you, our only concern is to rescue your little son.'

Maurice found his voice and was aware that this spider had said he was here to save Joseph. 'How, how can you save my son from such a l- large cat?' Maurice spoke with some difficulty.

The spider smiled, a kind sort of smile. (Yes, spiders can smile!) 'You just stay here my friend and watch us.'

Maurice, rooted to the spot watched in amazement as the walls of the living room turned black with a mass of humming spiders moving swiftly towards the cat. The large cat never stood a chance. Before he had time to realise what was happening hundreds of crawling spiders of all sizes fell upon him as one. Swiftly, they began their work weaving their webs, over and over, under and under, round and round, releasing miles and miles of silver thread. Working like hundreds of black demons, until the cat was trapped in a tight paralysing cocoon.

Before Maurice had time to collect his thoughts and feelings, the black cloud had gone, leaving only the large spider beside Maurice. Maurice still a little uncertain of the spider, took a step backwards.

The spider, smiling to himself called to Joseph, 'Come out little one you are quite safe now.'

Joseph, finding the use of his tiny legs, rushed from under the sideboard into his father's open arms and there he stayed for some moments.

Maurice, becoming aware that his fear for this friend had gone for now he thought of the spider and all the others, as true friends who had saved his son's life.

'How can I ever thank you?' his voice was a little shaky. 'I owe you a great deal of gratitude, how can I ever thank you?'

Joseph, now recovering from his ordeal was eager to thank the spider for himself.

'Oh, thank you, thank you Mr Spider for saving me from that nasty old cat,' then remembering to add, 'and all your friends.'

The spider gave a deep chuckle. 'It was our pleasure and don't you worry about that cat anymore. If I am not mistaken it will be a long them before he will feel like hunting for mice again, if ever.'

Joseph, tugged his father's arm to pull him down so he could whisper in his ear.

As Maurice listened to his son, he nodded in agreement. 'My dear friend, I would like to endorse what my son has just suggested. He and my family would like very much for you all to dine with us very soon.'

The spider gave a small bow. 'It would give me great pleasure to accept your kind invitation. However I feel it would be impossible for you to entertain us all. Nevertheless, I would be delighted to accept your offer to dine with you.'

Maurice beamed, 'That would be wonderful, when can we look forward to your visit?'

Well dear reader I cannot give you the details of this dinner party, but I can tell you everyone had a wonderful time. It was a start of a lifelong friendship between Maurice and all the spiders.

Now let this be a lesson to us all. We will never know who our true friends in life are until we are in need of help!

DOWN AT THE BOTTOM OF JOSEPH'S GARDEN
Sarah Tyrrell

Joseph was now almost five years old and loved playing in the garden, no matter what weather it was. There was an old shed to go into where Joseph played happily with his toy kitchen and had plenty of pots and pans that his mummy had bought for him, Joseph called it Jo Jo's Cafe. Joseph and his mummy had only just moved into their new house so there was much work and tidying up to be done yet, and Joseph hadn't had the chance to make any new friends either. The garden was very long and very narrow indeed with a long piece of grass down the middle and carried on for miles, until it reached the highest stone wall you had ever seen, the bottom of the garden looked very mysterious and spooky and Joseph longed to venture into it.

At the bottom of the garden it was very overgrown full of leftover wood, bricks, overgrown weeds and bushes. Joseph was looking at the bottom of the garden and wondering what was underneath all that mess. He started to cautiously wander down the garden grass when his mummy came to the back door and shouted, 'Joseph don't you go near the bottom of the garden, it's not safe.'

'Huh, OK,' Joseph shouted back disappointed, and carried on staring at the garden whilst kicking the long grass with his feet.

Ring, ring, ring, ring!

'Oh that's the telephone, Joseph you be good while I get that,' his mummy shouted, 'and don't go too far into the garden, it's not safe yet.'

Quickly she rushed inside and accidentally shut the old kitchen door behind her. Joseph smiled and thought, *this is my chance, I will just have a quick look and then go back inside to Mum.* So Joseph started walking slowly at first but then he got more and more excited and his pace became quicker and quicker. Through the long grass, over a chopped down fence, over some very old stones, over a few left bin bags, past the brown conifers and some strange looking bushes, of which Joseph had never seen before, whilst dodging all the flies and spiders. *I'm not frightened* thought Joseph and carried on with his adventure.

Joseph got onto his hands and knees and crawled through the small gap in the overgrown bushes. A thorn suddenly stuck in Joseph's arm then another thorn and another. 'Ahhh!' Joseph screamed loudly and looked at his arm and there was a trickle of blood. He became scared and turned around to go back through these nasty bushes and back to his mum, but the bushes had seemed to have got thicker and mysteriously more overgrown; he grasped them with his hands to try and make a hole in them, so he could get out. This didn't work so he shook them frantically but as he did his hands got even more thorns in them. Joseph let go and fell onto his bottom and started to kick the bushes instead, but it was no use, Joseph realised he was trapped in the bottom of the garden.

Joseph became scared; he was all alone, cold and remembered he hadn't even had his dinner! He could hear his breathing get faster and faster, his hands and arms were sore and still bleeding and then Joseph began to cry.

'Hello little boy, don't cry,' said a tiny voice.

Joseph jumped back on his feet and stood very still, startled and amazed. Joseph looked around and thought to himself, who could have just said that. Joseph turned around expecting his mummy to be there but he couldn't see anyone, he was now wishing he had done as his mummy had said and stayed in the garden. So he decided to lie down on the broken branches and tried his best to keep away from the thorns that were sticking out. Joseph curled up into a ball and waited for his mummy to come and find him he closed his eyes and began to cry again, a moment later Joseph heard the voice again.

'Err hello there,' bellowed the voice, the voice was much louder and stronger this time. Joseph quickly opened his eyes and to his amazement was a large ant, with bright red boots and a helmet on; Joseph sat up quickly but this time he wasn't scared, he wiped his eyes and smiled.

'I said hello there young man,' shouted the ant, the ant was really speaking. Joseph laughed and could not believe what he was seeing.

'Err err hello Mr Ant, are you really talking to me?' asked Joseph.

'Yes of course I am,' replied the ant.

He had a very posh English voice and carried on shouting at Joseph. 'Well I was trying to teach the army to march but you have interrupted me,' the ant said back in a hasty voice.

'I'm so sorry but I am stuck in the bottom of the garden and can't get back home,' Joseph cried.

'Oh,' the ant paused, rubbed his head and thought for a moment.

'We have heard you crying little boy, if we help you get back home will you promise to bring us some sugar cubes every day?' asked the ant.

'Err yes,' replied Joseph happily, 'every day.'

'My name is Major the ant but just call me Major, I am in charge of this garden so you best be a good boy!'

'Yes, yes I will,' Joseph managed to say between his tears and all the excitement.

'But why are you still so sad?' asked the major.

'Well my mummy said I was not to come to the bottom of the garden and . . .'

'Ah yes,' said the major interrupting.

'But you didn't do as your mummy said did you? Now Mummies and Daddies know best. You know I have the same problem too, I tell my family not to go too near the house but what do they do? And to make it worse I have hundreds of ants to look after.'

Joseph couldn't get a word in so he sat and listened, the ant began marching from left to right and carried on talking to Joseph.

'The bushes in this garden are very overgrown, but they are here to protect our colony, if a stranger passes the bushes, for example you little boy, they turn from nice flowering bushes into horrible thorny bushes that can sting,' he said in a very army-like voice, which made Joseph jump.

'I know I have cut my arm and hands, I am very sorry Major,' Joseph said rather quietly. Joseph looked very sad and his eyes filled up with tears again. 'Will you help me please to get back to my house as my mummy will be cross with me?' Joseph asked the major.

'Well,' the major rubbed his head and replied, 'OK but this must be our secret and you must promise to bring the sugar every day!'

'Yes,' said Joseph and gave the ant a big smile.

The ant stood high on his back legs, marched up and down on the spot and took a deep breath in and shouted, 'Army of ants gather immediately!'

Just then the ground underneath Joseph seemed to tremble and Joseph looked confused.

'Don't worry,' said the major, 'it's just my family coming to help you out of here.'

All of a sudden there were hundreds of ants crawling down the wall, over the wood and stones, up from holes in the soil; and then all stood in an army-like line.

'Right, *attention!*' shouted the major.

All the ants marched all their feet and came to a standstill; the army of ants were standing silently and waited on their next instructions.

'Right this is Joseph from the house at the top of the garden, he came into our secret garden and is very sorry. If we take him back to his mummy he has promised to bring us sugar cubes every day, so what do we say?'

A great cheer and shouts of 'yes' came from the army of ants, but the major soon interrupted. 'But slight problem chaps, the bushes have overgrown behind Joseph and he can't get back without our help. So are we going to help him?' shouted the major.

'Yes Sir we will,' the army of ants cheered. Joseph smiled.

'Places please!'

All the ants scurried around the garden and worked together.

'Right Joseph lie down on your back and leave the rest to us!' the major instructed.

Joseph laid down on the uncomfortable bed of wood and stones, all he wanted was to go back to his mummy and fast. All of a sudden he felt his body being lifted slightly into the air; he realised that the ants were underneath him and were carrying him slowly underneath the tiny gap of the horrible overgrown bushes.

'Onwards ants!' cried out the major.

'1 2 3 4 . . . 1 2 3 4' was the chanting.

Slowly but surely Joseph was being taken underneath the bushes then over the dirty stones and rotten old wood with lots of rusty nails sticking out of them; over the rubbish and torn bin bags where a mouse was searching for scraps of food. He was that busy he didn't even see Joseph; past some of Joseph's old toy cars that he had lost, a few marbles and even some toy soldiers that even looked lost! Past the brown conifers and the horrible overgrown and thorny bushes and finally out the other side.

Joseph was back in his nice garden, the ants put him down on the soft grass and gathered in front of him, the major stood up and said, 'Well here you are young man, safe and sound.'

'Oh thank you, you are so kind to me, and very strong too, you are all my best friends,' Joseph said happily.

All the ants cheered and laughed. 'We have never had a little boy as a friend before,' cried one of the other ants.

The major put his hand up and everyone was quiet, 'Now remember Joseph what you promised,' said the major.

'I do,' said Joseph, 'I will bring you some sugar in the morning.'

Joseph then pulled out his pocket a half eaten chocolate bar and placed it on the grass, the ants quickly put it onto their backs and started disappearing back into the bushes. The major crawled up Joseph's leg onto his arm and whispered into his ear, 'If you want to visit us again you have to say this magic rhyme and the bushes will magically open up for you. It's, 'Garden, garden be so kind, let me come and play, with these new friends of mine'.'

'Oh thank you,' Joseph said.

The ant jumped back onto the grass and shouted to the remaining ants.

'OK army, let's move it. Move out!'

The ants marched quickly back into the undergrowth and disappeared, whilst Joseph stood and watched.

'Joseph, tea's ready!'

Joseph's mummy appeared at the back door. Joseph smiled and ran so fast back to the house and leapt into his mummy's arms and gave her a big cuddle, and his mummy kissed him on the head and looked at him and said, 'Joseph why are you so dirty and what have you been up to?'

'Nothing!' Joseph said and smiled and remembered his special day and couldn't wait for tomorrow's adventure.

THE BLACKBIRD
C R Parker

Just a few hours away, in the valley of dreams, lived a beautiful queen, her name was Isobela. Behind her palace lived an old woman. She lived on Red Crest Mountain. Isobela was a very jealous queen.

One day Pernickerty Pumpkin a long-legged jester, came to the palace and told Queen Isobela how he had heard the most beautiful singing coming from Red Crest Mountain. Queen Isobela was a vain person, but this news made her fly into a jealous rage.

After scheming for some time, Isobela decided she must find some way up the mountain to find out who it was who could sing so beautifully. She decided to consult Wizard Montgomery. Wizard Montgomery lived at the foot of Red Crest Mountain. He had heard the singing and knew it was the old woman's granddaughter. When the queen asked him he could tell no lie. He gave the queen a magic potion, so enabling her to turn her into a blackbird, thus enabling her to fly to where the old woman lived.

Swiftly the queen took the potion and as soon as she did she turned into a blackbird. She flew off into the mountain. Higher and higher she soared until she came to the old woman's house. Once outside she perched on the branch of a tree, and waited to hear the singing. Not long after arriving a young girl appeared out of the house. Her tawny hair cascaded down her back and she had the most beautiful face the queen had ever seen. Her eyes were the colour of the violets she was carrying, and she was dressed in the prettiest of blue dresses. She looked a picture in the morning sunshine.

Queen Isobela could only chirp like a sparrow. Young Martinette, for that was the maiden's name, saw the blackbird. She gave the bird some food and water. Then she sat on a log making daisy chains. As she sat there she started to sing. Every animal on the mountain stopped what they were doing and came close, so they could listen. Queen Isobela was taken with the girl's beauty. *Oh how I would love to be able to sing like that.*

Martinette saw that the bird was coming closer, and sensing that something was wrong asked the bird, 'Can I help you?'

Queen Isobela's spell was wearing off and her beak was changing into a nose.

'Oh you do look funny,' said Martinette.

Queen Isobela could speak by this time, and she asked Martinette if she would teach her how to sing. Martinette said that she would. So Queen Isobela stayed on Red Crest Mountain until she had learned how to sing.

When it was time to leave, Isobela took some more of the wizard's potion and turned back into the blackbird. What she did not know though was that she took too much, and instead of turning back into a queen, she stayed as a blackbird. She was happy because she could fly around but also she had the most beautiful singing voice in the world. As a matter of fact, if you listen very carefully you can hear her singing every spring and summer. She is a beautiful bird with a beautiful voice.

TEA TIME FOR TERRY TEA TOWEL
Elizabeth McNeil

'Oh dear,' said Mrs Tawny, 'it's almost five o'clock, my friend Barbara is coming to tea at half past five, I must get out some biscuits and that nice strawberry cake I bought today. I think I will bring out my best tea set, and I could use my new canteen of cutlery Barbara bought me for my birthday. It's such a lovely gift, with knives, forks, soup and dinner spoons, oh and those pretty little tea spoons.'

Just as Mrs Tawny had placed her tea set on the coffee table, Barbara her friend rang the doorbell, *good timing*, thought Mrs Tawny, *I have just put the kettle on to make the tea.*

As Mrs Tawny let Barbara in she asked her to come through to the kitchen, they could chat while Mrs Tawny poured the hot water into the teapot.

'I heard your sister is sick, is she better?' asked Barbara.

'Yes,' said Mrs Tawny, 'it was only a cold, but I did stay over for the night just to make sure she was all right as she lives on her own. Unfortunately I had left my washing out and it got soaking wet and filthy. I was so worried when I got home and went to fetch it in, because I couldn't find my lovely hand towels, I thought they had been blown away and lost forever in the terrible wind and rain.'

'If it hadn't been for clever little Terry Tea Towel I wouldn't have found them again.'

'Why whatever happened?' asked Barbara.

'Well,' said Mrs Tawny, 'when I saw that Handy and Andy the two hand towels were missing, I didn't realise that they had been blown around the back of the shed. It was only when Terry Tea Towel was caught by the wind and bravely tossed himself over and down behind the shed, where he laid himself by Handy and Andy the two hand towels that I was able to find them.'

'Oh what a lovely story,' said Mrs Tawny's friend, 'and what a brave little Terry Tea Towel he was, he could easily have been blown away himself.'

Mrs Tawny and her friend Barbara chatted away quite happily while they enjoyed the lovely strawberry cake and biscuits, and especially the tea, which they drank out of Mrs Tawny's best tea set. When they'd finished their tea Mrs Tawny put the dishes and cutlery into the kitchen sink with some water to soak while she and her friend carried on chatting. Mrs Tawny had also brought out Terry Tea Towel from the drawer and laid him next to the sink ready to use to dry the dishes.

'My what a lovely day why don't we go outside into the garden and enjoy the sunshine, the dishes can wait but the sunshine won't!' said Mrs Tawny to her friend.

As Mrs Tawny and her friend went outside, they didn't notice Fluffy Mrs Tawny's cat go into the kitchen, she was very hot and wanted a drink but Mrs Tawny hadn't noticed because she was too busy chatting to her friend.

Fluffy the cat wandered around the kitchen looking for something to drink, but as he didn't come inside very often he didn't have a bowl on the floor, his bowl was outside and very empty, Mrs Tawny had forgotten to refill it because she had been so excited at seeing her best friend Barbara.

Fluffy knew he wouldn't have a bowl of milk lying around the kitchen floor, but he knew where Mrs Tawny kept the milk, in the fridge which stood next to the sink, but of course he couldn't open the door while standing on the floor, so he jumped up onto the sink and thought to himself, *how easy it would be to step over the dishes and get to the fridge door.*

This was a disaster waiting to happen, because the sink was quite wet and poor Fluffy slipped head over heels into the sink full of water. There was water everywhere on the floor, all over the cupboards and even the kitchen curtains were soaked. But goodness me worse was still to come because Fluffy, who was terrified and struggling to get out of the water, knocked Mrs Tawny's best tea set to the floor and it broke into a hundred pieces.

Even Terry Tea Towel got wet and he hadn't dried one single cup, *oh not again, I'm soaking wet for the second time and I haven't even been used to dry the dishes, Mrs Tawny will be so angry*, thought Terry Tea Towel.

All this noise brought Mrs Tawny and her friend Barbara running in not knowing what to expect. As they rushed in, poor Fluffy the cat screeched squealed and made all sorts of terrified noises as he raced past the two friends.

'My goodness whatever is the matter with Fluffy?' yelled Mrs Tawny, 'I hope I haven't got a burglar and I do hope Fluffy is alright, I'm sure he was all wet when he ran past us, I wonder why?

'Oh no what a mess,' said Mrs Tawny when she ran into the kitchen, 'I can't believe what I am seeing, my lovely clean kitchen is wet from top to bottom,' but she was even more upset when she saw her beautiful tea set or what was left of it, lying in bits all over the kitchen floor. 'Surely Fluffy can't have caused all this damage?'

Poor Mrs Tawny was really upset and started to cry, her friend Barbara tried to comfort her and started to clean the kitchen, but Mrs Tawny was horrified when Barbara picked up Terry Tea Towel, wrung him out and started to wipe round everywhere.

'*Stop!* What are you doing? That's Terry Tea Towel you are using to wipe the mess up with,' yelled Mrs Tawny, 'you'll spoil him, it was him that found Handy and Andy the two hand towels, I could never use him as an old floor cloth!'

Barbara, Mrs Tawny's friend was upset now, she was only trying to help and had picked the nearest thing to wipe up the water, she didn't know that it was Terry Tea Towel, she was very sorry and apologised to Mrs Tawny, who by now had realised how horrible she had been to her friend Barbara and said sorry to her, they hugged each other and made friends again. Mrs Tawny and Barbara soon dried everything using floor cloths and picked up the pieces of her best tea set, her friend Barbara made Mrs Tawny feel better by telling her that she would buy her a new tea set. With all the water that the two friends had wiped up, they too were quite damp so Mrs Tawny brought out Handy and Andy the two hand towels.

'Here you are,' said Mrs Tawny to Barbara, 'meet Handy and Andy the two hand towels that Terry Tea Towel rescued, they are lovely and soft, you can use them to dry your hands on.'

When everything was cleared up Mrs Tawny put Terry Tea Towel, Handy and Andy the two hand towels and Slippy and Sloppy the floor cloths into the washing machine. 'Here we are again,' said Terry Tea Towel to Handy and Andy getting washed once more, that's all we seem to do laughed Terry Tea Towel.

'I suppose you lot think you were the only ones that cleaned up the kitchen,' scowled Slippy and Sloppy the floor cloths, 'aren't you forgetting who did the real work, the tough dirty work? Mrs Tawny got us out of the drawer because you lot are wimps and would fall apart if you had to wipe anything tougher than hands and dishes. You'd better watch out when we are being put into the drier you wouldn't like to get tangled up with us, we might spoil your pretty looks.'

Slippy and Sloppy threatening Terry Tea Towel and Handy and Andy made them very scared, they knew why Mrs Tawny kept them for best and didn't use them to wipe the floor. It was because they were still new, and anyway they were bought from a nicer shop than those smelly floorcloths Slippy and Sloppy. Terry Tea Towel wasn't going to tell them that, he was frightened enough of what Slippy and Sloppy were going to do.

The washing machine had stopped now, it had washed the towels and cloths, *oh no* thought Terry Tea Towel and Handy and Andy the two hand towels, *here comes Mrs Tawny to put us in the drier, Slippy and Sloppy will try and tangle us up and we could get ripped to pieces.*

Terry Tea Towel and Handy and Andy couldn't believe what happened next, Mrs Tawny opened the washing machine door and took out Terry Tea Towel, Handy and Andy the two hand towels and hung them over the clothes airer, 'I won't put my towels in the drier because it makes them hard and they will get creased. I will put the floor cloths in because it doesn't matter if they get creased, they'll get dry quicker and I can put them out of sight, because they don't look very nice.' Slippy and Sloppy weren't very pleased by what they heard, but they couldn't do much about it.

Terry Tea Towel, Handy and Andy the two hand towels didn't say anything, but they did smile to themselves and sighed with relief that nothing bad had happened. After all they'd had enough scary adventures to last them for a very long time. Soon the friends were all dry and ironed and put away safely.

A SPIRITED FRIENDSHIP
S Mullinger

Dull thud. Followed by another. Molly quickly sat up in bed, dropping her book onto the floor. Looking around in her torch's half light, she could not see anything. But Molly noticed her room had suddenly turned colder. Bravely she put on her bedside light. Peered over to the corner of the room, where packed boxes were stacked high against the wall. A loud whooshing sound was heard as her bedroom curtains began to sway back and forth - faster and faster. Molly leapt from bed, slipperless, fled to the safety of the old stone kitchen and Mum.

'Goodness me!' exclaimed Sally, 'whatever is the matter? Why are you clutching your torch? Hope you've not been reading scary stories after I said lights out.'

Molly waited for her mother to finish. Then blurted out, 'There's someone in my room. There were two loud noises, my curtains were moving, my room got colder. I know someone's in my room.' Molly's voice got louder and louder, until she shouted, 'I hate it here, want to go and live in London with Dad. Didn't want to move to this village. I've got no one to play with, please take me home.'

Molly's mum Sally, embraced her daughter as her rage ran its course. She did not rush upstairs because since moving into the cottage two weeks ago, this scene was repeated almost nightly. To reassure Molly, the first few times Sally had gone to investigate. Nothing was found when she entered the bedroom. Sally never heard any banging or saw the curtains move. Discussing the incidents with her recently divorced husband, Jim, it was decided that Molly was actively attention seeking. She had been very upset by their divorce and her move to the countryside. Plain to both parents that Molly felt excluded from the decisions they had made. This was now payback time.

Patiently Sally waited until Molly's tantrum finished. She gave her a glass of hot milk, took her back to bed. 'Light's out,' said Sally firmly, 'no more using your torch to read, it will damage your eyes and give you a headache.' After giving Molly a kiss, Sally left the room.

Poor Molly! It was obvious her mum did not believe her. Finally drifting off to sleep, she thought I must get some proof - then Mum will understand.

Early next morning, Molly aged nine, of Rose Tree Cottage became, Molly, private investigator. Searching through a large cardboard box she found a pen, old notepad and her camera. Placing these items beside her torch on the bedside table, went downstairs for breakfast. Her investigation would have to wait.

'We could walk to the shops today, buy you an ice cream,' suggested Sally.

'Alright,' replied Molly reluctantly, 'but hurry please as I have something to do, when we return.'

On the way to the village, Sally, stopped to talk to all her new neighbours. Bored, Molly began to look around her for the first time. Noticed the beautiful old buildings with large flowered gardens and small wooden gates. Molly could not see any children playing. Strange because it was the middle of school summer holidays.

'Mum,' interrupted Molly, 'where are all the children?'

The elderly lady speaking to her mum replied, 'There's only Ryan, who lives at the farm. He's a good lad - helps his dad during holidays.'

'How old is he?' Molly asked.

'He's almost ten, expect if you pay a visit he'll be pleased to see you. His mum died when he was a baby and I hear he often gets lonely. Too far to walk into town to meet up with his school friends every day.'

'Have they got animals on the farm?' pestered Molly.

'Yes, cattle and sheep,' the lady answered.

Perhaps, thought Molly, *Mum would take her on a visit to the farm tomorrow.* She knew her mum would work on her paintings in the afternoon. Rich people paid Sally to paint pictures from photographs they sent.

Feeling happier, Molly skipped down her garden path, remembered and stopped abruptly. Time to investigate, which meant going to her room. Climbing the stairs, Molly felt nervous. Peering round the door, shouted, 'I'm back.' Walked inside and uttered a silent scream as she looked into the black eyes of a girl watching her.

'You can see me, I am here,' calmly said the black-eyed one.

'Who are you? How did you get into my room?'

'My name's Ruth, same age as you, I've heard your mum call you Molly. I live here, have done for ages.'

Trying hard not to stare at the old-fashioned clothes Ruth was wearing, Molly said, 'Don't be silly, Mum and I live here.'

'No, not now,' replied Ruth, 'what year is it?'

'It's August twentieth, two thousand and two, this cottage belongs to us,' stated Molly.

'Yes,' answered Ruth, 'but in nineteen hundred and two the cottage belonged to my parents.'

'Who moved my camera?' Noting it was now placed on the floor. *A strange girl in my bedroom,* thought Molly - no need to investigate further, this explained everything! 'Was it you who made the loud noises?'

'Yes,' responded Ruth, 'I haven't mastered walking through walls properly. Oh! I also made the curtains sway. Tried to let you know I was around.'

Molly surmised, *either this girl mad or I have got my very own . . . ghost.* 'If you've been here all the time, why couldn't I see you until today?' asked Molly.

Ruth stated that she tried to get Molly to notice her before but at night Molly ran downstairs in fright. During the day Molly did not usually go to her room. Curious, Molly demanded to know if Ruth lived at Rose Tree Cottage as a baby.

'Yes, I was born here in nineteen hundred and two.'

'But that makes you a hundred years plus,' Molly laughed.

'No,' exclaimed Ruth, 'and you think I'm silly, I died of a fever in nineteen hundred and eleven. I'll always be nine.'

Molly called to her mum.

'No!' Ruth shouted, 'No!'

Molly felt a cold sensation as Ruth disappeared. When Sally reached the room, she found Molly, looking pale, hot and feeling sick.

The local doctor suggested bed rest for the remainder of the day. How could she tell her mum about Ruth? Molly knew Sally would not believe her. There must be someone she could ask about her personal ghost. Like why did she have one? Why was the girl haunting her? *Bet a living ghost was not mentioned to Mum before she bought the cottage,* thought Molly as she drifted off to sleep - the effect of the tablets given to her by the doctor.

Next morning Molly felt better and begged to be taken to the farm to meet Ryan. The visit was a great success. Molly and Ryan instantly became friends. She enjoyed seeing the animals. Mum suggested they could stay longer next time, pleased to see a smile on her daughter's face.

Returning home, Molly ran ahead of Sally. Glancing up, she stopped as she saw Ruth standing at her bedroom window. Angrily Molly climbed the stairs and asked Ruth what she thought she was doing. 'Why can't my mum see you?' questioned Molly.

'Because she's a grown-up, only children can see me, in the right circumstances. You see I can't leave this house yet' Ruth answered. 'One day when my job is done, I will go but I chose to stay when I died. It was where I felt happiest. My task is to see that any sad, lonely child who lives here, grows into a happy adult with my encouragement.'

'I don't understand,' said Molly, 'why you have to do a job when you're dead.'

'Well I suppose it's like gaining knowledge,' Ruth continued. 'All children who die early are given a list, if they want they choose a task to perform. It could have been looking after sick animals when their owners were away, or visiting older people to keep them company. But I like the company of children and thought I could help to improve their lives. For many years, only adults lived at Rose Tree Cottage. I could not help anyone. Then about four years ago, I was needed for the first time in my role as a helper. A young boy moved in but he didn't live here long enough for me to complete my job. Molly, you are sad and I'd like to help you but you speak harshly to me.'

'Molly, time for tea,' called Sally.

'Okay Mum!' shouted Molly. Molly left her room, thinking about Ruth, a ghost who wanted to befriend her.

'You alright sweetheart?' asked Sally. 'You'll be seeing Dad next weekend, he's taking you to London.'

'Could you ask him to collect me another time, I've lots to do here.'

'Fine darling,' replied Sally, amazed by Molly's words. 'I'll phone Dad later and explain.' Sally, drinking her tea, thought this could turn out to be a good move for her and for Molly.

'Do you think Ryan would like to come to tea tomorrow?' Molly inquired.

'Good idea! I'll ring the farm once I've done the washing up,' Sally stated.

Molly went for a walk in the garden, sitting down on the stone wall, she thought Ruth had said only children could see her. If Ryan could, then she would know she was not going mad. Then she'd decide what to do about her.

Tea over, Molly and Ryan asked to be excused. As they arrived in Molly's room, Ruth through the wall appeared. Ryan was not surprised. He said, 'Oh Ruth! Had forgotten about you.' Ryan told Molly he had met Ruth four years ago. Sid had lived at the cottage and Ryan visited. But being younger then, he had thought Ruth was Sid's older sister. Ryan explained that the three children had played together daily. The down side was that Ruth could not go outside. But then Sid's family moved away. An elderly couple moved in. There was no reason for Ryan to visit.

Later on it had all seemed so unreal. Only recently Ryan had looked into the background of the cottage at the library. The family who lived at Rose Tree Cottage in nineteen hundred and two had one daughter called Ruth. She had died of a fever aged nine. Her parents remained at the cottage until their own deaths believing Ruth had never left.

'Ruth, didn't you say something about cheering up a miserable child,' Ryan remarked, 'once that's done you will move on. Molly and I are both sad and lonely, can you make us both happy?'

Molly suggested, 'The only way for that to happen is for Ryan to come here every day.'

'Easily solved,' Ruth revealed, 'school starts soon, he can see you home, we can play together.'

Each evening Ryan visited Molly's home. Her gloom began to lift. Ryan no longer felt lonely. The three friends were a team, hours of laughter echoed round Molly's room. Ruth told the others popular tales of her childhood. Ryan told Ruth what he had learnt at school and Molly played music on the radio, to which they could dance. Neither Ryan or Molly mentioned Ruth to their parents. Certainly never mentioned her to other children in case they were laughed at or worse bullied. Ruth was their secret.

As the years passed, Ryan and Molly's friendship deepened. Throughout high school most of their spare time was spent at the cottage. In time, the wedding of Ryan and Molly was announced. Each arrangement was made with input from nine-year-old Ruth, whose childlike decisions delighted them all.

Wedding day came to a close. Molly, eighteen years old - had never looked happier. The newlyweds arrived to collect their luggage for their honeymoon. Ruth's job was complete, she was also leaving. But our two lovers, would always be grateful to their very own friendly ghost.

SILVER DUST WINGS

Jacquie Williams

Brandon was a charming child, with blond hair and blue eyes. He spoke politely and was praised for his gentle manner. But, beneath his angelic exterior there lay, undiscovered, a nasty streak, a streak of cruelty, oh, not to everything, just to creatures with wings.

It all started one day when his father opened his treasure chest, his chest of memorabilia from his army days.

Brandon's eyes lit up as he gazed into the chest. Inside stored neatly, though smelling of mothballs, lay his uniform and medals, grenades, guns, old photographs of army buddies and a large white silk box.

His father handed him a grenade to hold, explaining how it was harmless now that the explosive and pin were disarmed. Brandon rubbed the tip of his nail over each groove cut into the metal, but all Brandon wanted to see was the silk box.

'What's in the box Daddy, can I see?'

'Yes in a minute, I thought you would enjoy looking through my old army things now you are growing up.'

'Daddy, I am just ten you know.'

'I know you are son but I waited until you reached double figures, because you know one day I will handing all this down to you.'

'That's good Daddy, but can I see that box?'

'Patience Brandon, I thought a lad of your age would love to hear old war stories, you know there's a story about each piece of equipment here.'

Brandon's eyes were still fixed on the box. His father picked it up, it was the size of a school exercise book but a little thicker, the white silk was tied with string, parcel-like.

Brandon waited impatiently as his father slowly untied the box; he took a deep breath and gasped in awe when the lid finally came off. For lying silently on the soft, white wadding, was the biggest winged insect he had ever seen.

'Wow, Daddy, what is it? Can I hold it? Let me see, closer, closer!' said Brandon, pulling at the box.

'Hold on a minute Brandon,' his father took the box out of the boy's shaking hands, 'it's very delicate, if you slow down I will tell you what it is.'

Brandon sat down next to his father, eager for an explanation.

'Now this pretty creature is called a tiger moth.'

'A moth,' gasped Brandon, 'but it's so big.'

'Yes, now let me finish. It comes from another country, you can see the big, round spots on its wings, like an extra pair of eyes, it would give another predator a shock if he saw eyes as big as those.'

'Ooh, can I touch it Daddy?'

'Yes but carefully, it's very old.'

Brandon gently put his finger on the moth's wing, it left a trace of fine silver powder on his fingertip. He noticed that through the belly of the creature, like a stake, protruded a pin. *So that's how they killed it,* thought Brandon. He could not take his eyes off the creature, he felt no pity, only excitement. He wanted more of them, more trophies like these. To have a room filled with them, pinned all over the walls, he shook with anticipation, but how could he catch them?

'Daddy, how did you catch the tiger moth?' he asked innocently.

'Well now, that was a story, you see moths will fly towards a light or flame and this one night we had a blackout. The only light we had was a candle perched on an orange box while the guys played cards in our tent. Suddenly the candle started flickering and out of nowhere it flew at us. We ducked and dived, thinking it was some kind of bat, a bloodsucker maybe, so we grabbed whatever we could to hit it down. My buddy, Joe, hit it first but it flew back up, then I caught it with an old magazine, it fell to the floor. Tom got that old hat pin from his tin and stabbed the poor beggar through its stomach. He pinned it to his bed; do you know it was still flapping its wings over an hour later? Yes it took such a long time to die, I felt quite sad for it. But you know what lads are like, after a couple of beers, we played cards for it, guess who won?'

'You did Daddy and now he's mine . . . isn't he?' Brandon looked up at his father with pleading eyes.

'Alright, you can keep it, but why do you want it?'

'To show my friends,' answered Brandon quickly. He smiled with glee as he carried the box to his bedroom. This was better than burning ladybirds in a matchbox any day, oh it's fun when they crack, it's even more fun when they stretch those little birds' necks till they crack too, but moths, they will stay the same forever and . . . he sniffed the moth. *They don't smell either. Yes I must get myself more of these,* Brandon thought.

That night he left his bedroom window open wide and the light full on. He waited and then he heard a light strumming noise. In flew his first victim, it bounced on and off the light bulb, then onto the wall, then back to the light. Brandon watched and waited for it to settle. It landed on a shelf and beat its wings slowly as if trying to get its breath. With cupped hands, Brandon crept up to it. He caught it and felt it thrash itself against the skin of his hands trying to escape. He tried to hold it gently, but the temptation to squash his hands together was too much. He squeezed until the little creature became still. When he opened his hands the moth split in two, one of its wings stuck to his left palm and its body and wing stuck to the other. *Damn,* he thought, he rubbed his hands together in temper, bits of moth fell to the floor like confetti, but left on his hands like blood, was a silver, shiny powder.

More creatures mesmerised by the light flew in through the window. Brandon remembered the little fishing net under his bed. He dived on the floor and rummaged for it. He found it and an old sweet jar. *Great,* he thought, *I can catch them, collect them in a jar then skewer them with pins from Mum's sewing box, I wonder how long they will take to die?* Overcome with excitement he shook as he opened the sweet jar, then busied himself with catching moths in his net. It was almost dawn when he finished his task, the jar was filled with fluttering moths and silver powder stained the inside of the jar. He made a few small holes in the lid for them to survive, because he wanted them alive when he arrived home from school.

At school everyone looked at the silken box, some were afraid, others laughed, his teacher stood back in disgust, but Brandon relished it all. He loved the fearful expressions on the girls' faces, especially when he told them the story of how *he* had conquered the mighty tiger moth.

He rushed home from school, rummaged through his mother's sewing box, found the pins, then hurried to his room. He pulled the jar from beneath his bed and watched almost drooling as the trapped moths beat their wings. He thought he could hear them breathing. Perhaps they were pleading with him for their freedom. He laughed as he dipped his hand into the jar and captured one; quickly he replaced the lid. He held the first moth by its wings, gently at the tip, so it could not flap. He stared into its large eyes, then took a pin and stabbed it straight through the abdomen. Did it scream? Was that a scream? No, it must be children outside, he sneered and anyway, it would be much more exciting if it screamed louder. He timed it to three minutes to death and watched, dreamlike, as its wings beat slower and slower, then stopped. One by one he killed them and pinned them to a cork message board, with the tiger moth spread out in the middle. He could not measure the satisfaction he felt, his hands shone with silver dust, the more he rubbed them the more they shone.

His mother called him to have his tea, he had to tear himself away from his trophies, but tonight he would catch more and more. So he did, soon the mangled remains of moths filled his room, some he thought were quite pretty and others a dull brown colour. These he would torture the most. He still could not find one as big or as glorious as the tiger moth.

After a couple of weeks he grew bored with his moth torture and decided instead to go outdoors and pull the wings off a few dung beetles.

His mother took this opportunity to clean his room. When she entered she screamed in terror and disgust, calling for Brandon's father. His parents were in shock at his wanton cruelty.

When Brandon arrived home his parents told him of their disgust, they tried to instil in him some recognition of the bad he had done, but Brandon sat with his arms folded, pinching himself so he would not laugh at them.

Eventually he sighed, 'Mummy . . . Daddy, I am really sorry, I only wanted to catch another tiger moth. I will take them all down.' He then changed the tone of his voice to a quiver as if to cry, 'I promise I won't do it again.'

His parents of course believed him, but he had no intention of stopping his cruel games. He would take the moths down, maybe.

That night he slept restlessly, he dreamed of moths flying at him, he fought them off, but then as if he were the flame, a huge moth beat itself against him. He felt suffocated, trapped. Just as a huge stake almost pierced his abdomen, his father's face appeared. 'Brandon, wake up, wake up, you are having a bad dream, look at you all cocooned in your sheet, you must have been fighting with the Devil.'

Next morning Brandon took all his trophies down off the walls. He put them in a box and took them to the bottom of the garden, setting fire to them, he watched as the silver flames danced in the air. He thought he heard sighs of freedom, but he laughed it off and kicked the box. A beetle scurried past him, he glanced at it casually, then lifted his foot and crunch. *Oh, such satisfaction,* he thought as he twisted his foot from side to side until the little creature was annihilated. That night, after supper he entered his room and gazed around the empty walls with a twisted sorrow, but he still had one skewered to the corkboard, his tiger moth. He pulled the window almost shut just leaving a small gap so some air could get in on this warm summer night. For a while he stared at his moth, rubbing his fingers on its wings just to feel the silky, silvery powder between his fingers, then yawning and stretching, he crawled into bed.

That night his mother called in to check on him. He was sleeping soundly, the room seemed a little stifling so she opened his window wide, then looking at him one more time, she crept out, closing the door quietly behind her. Amidst the darkness a light, dim at first, emulated from the tiger moth, then it seemed to hum and beat until the light became almost luminous. Through the window came a mighty rush of wind, then a humming louder as the moths happily and hungrily got on with their work, flapping and spinning in an organised, almost erotic eager togetherness. At dawn the room became silent and a cockerel crowed out a new day in a distant farmyard.

Brandon's mother had almost exhausted her voice calling him for school; she became so irritated when he did not answer that she decided to go to his room to wake him. As she opened the door, silver rain greeted her on shafts of sunlight that shone through the window. She walked over to Brandon's bed to wake him, but all she found was a silver shadow draped with strings of silken thread. She thought she heard someone whisper and a warm breeze brush past her face. But what she felt was the silent beating of a thousand fluttering silver dust wings.

Brandon was never found.

PIERROT LOVE
Fiona Gunn

Hi, my name is Aimee; I am 13 and-a-bit years old. I live in Opeltown with my mum, dad and two little brothers, Colin and Euan and tonnes of pet rabbits. I have blonde, curly hair, blue eyes; I am quite small with small feet. My ears are pierced but my nose is not. I think my teeth are nice. This is my diary; you are welcome to read it.

16/04/83 (Mermaid me)

Today I went to the shops with Leanda and Sophie. I bought this diary and a rubber from Ink Blots. I had a grape-flavoured Slush drink. My rubber is shaped like a packet of mints.

It's splashing time for me today. I went to the swimming baths. I can swim quite well now. I have only 3p left out of £3.55. I need 10p for going to the Youth Club.

Mum's going to buy Scotch pies for me and Dad's going to buy chips from the chip shop.

Had a good day. My folk's friends, Elspeth and John are going to visit at 9pm. No *Kidz Fame* doubles in my sticker book so far.

I owe Mum 50p. It's pouring with rain.

PS: Leanda and Sophie went to the baths with me.

17/04/83 (Calamity Jane, that's my name!)

Today was the Girls' Brigade Divisional Parade. When Mum was making my packed lunch she asked me to climb up to the high cupboard to get crisps down. I accidentally pulled a pot plant all over myself. There was soil and plant and pot all over my nice white shirt. Calamity! However, I cleaned it off and went to Sunday school. I was almost there when I remembered I'd left my silly hat behind.

Second calamity; Dad said he would get it and bring it in to me. I had my lunch in the church hall then we went to our parade in Rogoke.

I planted some seeds tonight (Livingstone daisies and something I can't remember).

18/04/83 (Age of tight jeans)

My school has been vandalised. The blackboards have been scribbled on, desks have been turned over, ink spilt on jotters.

It was Parents' Association AGM tonight. Mum, Dad and Euan went. Colin played on his bike and I walked around the block. I was cold.

I walked up to the school. I met Colin and the nice, chatty janitor (Janny), Mr Allon who let us sit indoors out of the cold.

Pretty uneventful day. I have cold feet.

PS: Mum took my jeans in, they are really nice and tight.

19/04/83 (Free freedom)

No more looking after the wee kids at school. Time for peace. Started my French project today. Netball day is now Wednesday. Mrs Marsh talked about Dad's quick action. Sorry, I didn't tell you about that.

The Prestons were at our house for supper, they were leaving at 1am on Sunday, when the school bell started ringing. Dad went over and he saw 2 girls coming down the path carrying a white polythene bag. He stopped them.

They said, 'Er . . . it was the boys up at the back of the school.' Then they burst past Dad. Dad called the police and they caught them with the loot. They had vandalised the inside of the school.

20/04/83 (Ugly mugs)

Today I got in a row with Mrs Marsh. I was only looking at my book, she thought I was talking to Anne. I went back to my seat. Everyone started talking to me about it. I felt tears coming to my eyes, one ran down my cheek and onto my glasses.

My friend Carol was the only one who noticed. She said, 'What's wrong?'

I said nothing.

Pain-in-the-butt Douglas Cardton, mocking me said, 'Rubber.'

I muttered, 'Shut your gaggy.'

We wrote an essay on our favourite TV programme. I did Grange Hill. (Nice)

Alice McFall is the gala queen. Judy and not so pretty Sarah Weston are attendants. Yuck! I'll never hear the end of this with Sarah.

21/04/83 (Busy Lizzy)

I have been very busy lately. My room is a disaster. When I was woken up this morning, I didn't want to get up.

I went to the baths with the school today. I am in the breadth swimmers. I had Girls' Brigade tonight. I had a mad rush to get, 'Every day with Jesus' finished. I had to do about 16 days at once. I had no time to study school work.

I finished making the bread basket at Girls' Brigade. I missed Kidz Fame on TV again.

All in, a boring day. I bought an Aero (20p). My room is a pigsty but I'm too tired out. I really can't stand Gillian and Linda. Test tomorrow. Better go to sleep, see ya, *Aimee x x x*

22/04/83 (Dopey disco)

Got 43/45 in the maths test. *Carless! Careless even!* I'm still in the top group though.

I went to a play scheme disco. I knew it would be rubbish before I went. There were wee kids running everywhere. Julie and I undid Lorna's bra. Then Lorna and I undid Julie's bra. They didn't do it to me but I was on the lookout.

The records were rubbish, so was the DJ. The whole thing was a disaster. Mrs Sealy the choir lady wants a bunny for her son Jamie. I am doing a solo. I have to practice in front of a mirror. I am worn out. Room's still a mess.

I want to sleep for 10 days. But I can't unfortunately.

PS: My friend Caroline got her mum to take in her jeans (copycat) not fair, cheater. I do not like people copying me, these are *my* ideas, all mine!

23/04/83 (Euro song)

I went to the baths and library. I went to the store for sweets for the Eurovision Song Contest. I got a small Dairy Milk and fudge. I ate the Dairy Milk. I made a blackcurrant and cider Slush Puppy. I had a jam sandwich and a cheese sandwich, a cup of fresh orange. The contest lasted 2 hours.

Alex and Morag visited Mum and Dad so I had the telly upstairs. Luxembourg won. I didn't like it much. Britain was great! Sweet Dreams singing Never Give It Up.

Prince William can crawl and has teeth. Wow he's amazing, like we don't all grow teeth! Prince Charles calls him Wills - daft I think!

Sweet Dreams are great!

24/04/83

Mum told me about her stage acting. She didn't get a fright the stage did! (I want to go for an audition but I want to go to stage school).

Colin took out the middle of a book. He's turned spy. Mum and I decided to trick him. We thought about it. We got a plastic fly. I showed it to Mum, she screamed and I dropped it. I put it in the book but took it out and threw it at Mum. She said, 'Where is it?'

I pointed to her arm, she looked, screamed and shook it off. We had a good laugh after our shock.

25/04/83

Scribbled out page.

26/04/83

Beat St Anne's at netball. Close game. Want deodorant. Too embarrassed to ask Mum. Going to try to ask her.

Went to Gillian's with Angela, she has a rope swing. Sometimes it goes into the big tree, you have to stop yourself from banging into it by pulling your feet out.

I am getting things from the catalogue. They add up to £60.93 but I might not keep them all. They look very nice.

Gym tomorrow. Taking wool to school to weave a scarf.

27/04/83 (Fit not fat)

Mrs Edwards is picking a netball team for the gala day. Chamois Primary School only. We will play all the teams on our school league. I hope I am picked for WA (wing attack).

I am on a diet.

I have started weaving at school.

Can't wait for the summer.

I am going swimming tomorrow.

I am exhausted after netball and badminton.

Youth Club tuck shop, the usual rubbish. All penny things, 'cept for the Topic bars were 15p. I only had 10½p with me.

I'm looking forward to the gala day.

28/04/83 (Up, Up, Up I Grow)

Went swimming today. Lorna, Jayne, Juleps and I wore our bras. Lorna brought the wrong size. A 28 and she takes a 30. However, she managed.

People are going in for the swimming gala. I'm not.

Mum bought me a deodorant.

I went to GB.

I got an exam. Caroline missed it.

Received photos today. They are good.

Brought weaving home to do.

Doing well on diet. Did exercises.

Life rather dull. GB display soon.

Choir tomorrow.

Room a disaster. Dad wrote a notice on the door. Something like; danger, disaster ahead, bomb about to explode or a buffalo attacking. You have been warned.

Auntie Helena had a baby boy. She called him Barry. He is a very small baby. Her other son, Craig, came today. He is 4.

Untidy today. Room a mess.

Sang in front of choir.

Got things from the catalogue.

Got school video home. Getting a film tomorrow.

Craig went to visit his mum and baby Barry.

I had to start my weaving again.

Going to tidy and clear out my room tomorrow.

Going to the baths.

Off on Monday, hooray!

Hair in middle parting. Finger next to pinkie on my right nail has gone square.

01/05/83 (Sorry, forgot)

I forgot to write in my diary for 2 days.

We got the school's video on 30/04/83, we got 'Airplane' (a comedy) and 'Watership Down' for Saturday 31/04/83. They were good.

Mr Blegg is leaving our church. He is going to America. The congregation are upset about this. He was asked 2 years ago but turned it down. He has been asked again. God is calling. No one wants him to go, but it is God's will (He knows best). Hmm? He will have someone prepared for us.

We got a stupid animal cartoon and Kramer Vs Kramer (it was great) I was almost in tears.

02/05/83

Aunt Helena got out of hospital today. Uncle Kenny came for dinner.

I'm busy working out my money. Thinking of ways to earn it. How to spend it.

It is Mum's birthday on Sunday 8th May. I don't know what to get her.

Back to school tomorrow.

I pulled out the tooth with the filling. Dad gave me 20p.

It is pouring with rain. I posted 4 letters.

Had a lazy day, watched Kramer vs Kramer again. Doesn't seem like Monday.

Holly, Caroline's dog's birthday is on the same day as Mum's.

03/05/83 (I am me!)

Why am I me? I have often wondered. God made me, but why am I me? Lorna, Wendy, Gillian and I are playing in the netball game tomorrow. Steven fancies Joanne because Lorna doesn't like him anymore. I don't know why Steven likes Jo, there are plenty of other, nicer girls.

Jayne has started her periods.

I broke my thread in weaving.

Not feeling well. Sore head, sore head, sore neck and a sore tummy.

Julie and I are planning a summer activity group. We will go to the baths, picnic, bike rides etc. This is to save us getting bored in the summer holidays.

I get 'Girlz' magazine delivered tomorrow.

Room is a disaster. I think I'll clear it out. Thought this about 2 weeks ago, but I never did it.

THE NINTH GRANDCHILD
Carolyn A Smith

Penny had some wonderful dreams, so many that she couldn't remember them all. But she did recall the haunting, strange, soft music she seemed to hear in the background, which never grew any louder and never faded away.

It awoke her each morning too and made her hours of daylight play as enchanted as her fairy dreams. Penny danced through the mornings and hummed gaily through the afternoons and still the music never grew louder nor faded away. It was her bedtime lullaby and carried her on the fantasy of beautiful sleep into the lands even fairytale books could never picture! When she retold their stories to her mother and mentioned the weird, endless melody that wove its way through every silence and brightened her daytime play like a never setting sun, Penny's mother said that even she, as a girl, could not remember anything so curiously wonderful!

However, she did know someone who could! Penny went to ask her grandma if she could explain it and listened with rapt attention to Grandma's tale of happy childhood near the summer meadows at the edge of the nearby woods.

'You are the ninth grandchild of a ninth grandchild.' Grandma replied mysteriously, her kind, smiling green eyes sparkling as if touched with magic. 'Nine is a very special number. We are privileged children of nature my dear and you are just beginning to experience the first of many mysterious and beautiful things in your ninth year.'

Penny was terribly eager to learn about the other wonderful things that would happen too! But Grandma bid her be patient. A finger on her granddaughter's lips, she made a sign: 'Time will bless you, my little Penelope. Let the fairy folk charm your days until you are ten and you will never forget . . .'

Penny sensed a silvery shimmer around her, a gentle, distant ringing charmed her ears. 'Ooh!' she gasped, breathless with wonder and excitement. What did Grandma mean?

The smile on the old lady's face twinkled and as Penny sat on the oak wood stool in Grandma's kitchen, the elfin melody suddenly seemed to grow louder and louder until she felt surrounded by an orchestra so big that it stretched as far as she could see in all directions, beyond the walls of the cottage kitchen to the meadows and to the woods. Grandma's voice was a song in that music, still telling its strange story and carrying Penny along as if on air.

Suddenly, Penny was standing at the edge of the woods, holding Grandma's hand very tightly! The music faded to its soft haunting murmur. Her eyes opened wider and wider! Was this really happening?

'Now,' whispered Grandma's voice, 'go into the woods and let the music take you where it will. Do not try to resist - or the spell will be broken. Do not try to follow a different path - there is only one for we special folk.'

Penny watched in silent amazement as Grandma's finger made a graceful sign to the rhythm of the music . . . and Grandma was no longer there.

'Grandma?' she called, quietly, gazing around. 'Go Penelope, don't be afraid,' came the old lady's voice. 'I am not far away and will bring you home. Until then . . .'

Penny felt the strange melody take control of her, leading her through unknown avenues of richly green summer trees and flowers coloured as brightly as sunlight and they all seemed to be a note in that enchanted melody.

Then, quite unexpectedly, the world appeared upside-down and the sky was beneath her small feet, dark blue as midnight.

Penny was the haunting music, each step she took a ringing echo that vibrated softly through the leaves, returning even louder. Just like her marvellous dreams!

Her feet stopped. She smiled happily, not at all afraid, She recognised *this* woodland glade where many night-time hours had led her.

Do dreams *really* come true?

'Look!' rustled the leaves in gentle notes . . .

'Listen!' whispered the grass in its soft, swishing song . . .

Penny looked and the fallen midnight grew bluebells all around her, stretching far away beyond the trees and the trees were of crystal, glinting sunlight tinkling with musical echoes.

Penny listened and that strange, haunting music rang out from every flower, not growing louder nor fading away.

Penny, ninth grandchild of a ninth grandchild, had taken part in the ballet of the woods on midsummer's day.

Mr Fuzzy Rabbit Wigglebottom
Janet Middleton

Fuzzy Rabbit Wigglebottom hopped across the field. 'Nice day Horace,' he said to Horace the pony. His white, fluffy tail wiggled.

'Neigh, neigh, same to you Fuzzy.'

Fuzzy Wigglebottom went on across the field, hopping, tail wiggling, through the gate, down to the stream for a drink of water. Fuzzy's ears went up, listening for danger. 'I hope those nasty ferrets aren't about, they'd eat me.'

'Where are you going Wigglebottom?'

Shaking water off, Fuzzy looked up. In the tree was Mr Goldie Eagle.

'Mr Goldie Eagle, good day to you. I'm looking for a new place to live. Our burrow is being torn up, big people building in our field.'

'Sad, sad it is, open fields and meadows seem to be going away fast, but all is not lost. No, now, some places will still be green with wild flowers - buttercups! Over that hill you should find a place to suit you!'

'Thank you Mr Goldie Eagle,' replied Fuzzy Wigglebottom, 'good day.' On and on Fuzzy hopped, bottom wiggling, his legs were getting tired, he was ready to sleep.

The hill Mr Eagle spoke of seemed a long way off. Finding a hole in a tree, Fuzzy sniffed and sniffed, ears up, it looked empty. 'This will have to do for tonight,' he said. Carefully, Fuzzy went in the tree hole, Moving his body about he got cosy. He rolled up into a fuzzy ball and fell fast asleep.

Fuzzy Wigglebottom dreamed of loads and loads of wild flowers, grassy meadows and blue skies.

In the morning he woke to a lot of chirping and rustling leaves. 'What is going on?'

Two squirrels were playing chase up and down the tree.

'Can't you keep quiet? It's much too early,' Fuzzy said, poking his head out.

'Good morning Mr Rabbit, what is your name?'

'It's Fuzzy Wigglebottom. What are your names?'

They giggled squeakily and replied, 'Fred and Freda Squirrel.'

Fuzzy Wigglebottom lived up to his name, when he got angry or upset, his bottom wiggled! His little white tail bobbed and bobbed as it was doing now. Fuzzy rubbed his eyes, peeked outside the tree. 'Far too noisy, must find somewhere quieter. Goodbye Freda and Fred, I'm on my way, on my way, on my way to find my place where I want to stay hey, hey.'

Leaving the squirrels Fuzzy had to pass a farm! Dogs! They chased rabbits like him. 'Oh no,' Fuzzy's tail went bob, bob, bob, creeping past the dogs out into the next field and the next, as fast as his legs would go. Mr Fuzzy didn't stop, 'I must get away from those dogs. Oh my, oh my! What if there are foxes, they're like those dogs!' His heart thumped.

'Don't worry, I'm here,' said a voice, 'look up,' Mr Goldie had been watching over Fuzzy!

'I forgot you eagles too eat rabbits,' Fuzzy said.

'I'm not going to eat you, I don't have a family to feed, I like fish better!' said Goldie.

'Thank goodness,' Fuzzy let out a whoosh.

'Okay, next field you'll be home.'

And sure enough, over the hill Fuzzy Wigglebottom saw a wonderful sight. Rabbits playing, jumping, feeding, blue skies,

'Hello, you're looking for a new home? My name's Fluffy.'

'My name's Wigglebottom, and yes I am.' said Fuzzy, 'Is there a spare burrow for me?'

'I'm sure we can find you one,' Fluffy said.

Fluffy took him along by the stream, up through the very long grass in the middle of the field, then down a big tunnel into Rabbit City.

One burrow was next door to Fluffy's. 'You can have this one if you like.'

Fuzzy's tail was still. It was big, roomy and safe! 'Thank you, Fluffy.'

It was quiet, loads and loads of fields, flowers, clover, long grass outside, and nobody building on it. Fuzzy knew he was home.

THE LITTLE ROSEBUD
Sally-Anne Hardie

The sun was shining warmly on the rich brown earth and all the little insects that lived there were scurrying about - tiny brown beetles were popping back and forth among the small stones, while the beautiful butterflies hovered over the flowers which were slowly opening up their petals as the sun coaxed them awake. Even the big bumblebee could be heard humming busily as he searched for his early morning breakfast of honey. He and the butterfly both enjoyed the same food which they got from the flowers.

Whilst all this early morning activity was going on a little rosebud was very, very slowly unfurling her tiny petals for the first time. All through the cold winter she lived off the goodness her parent bush had given her. The man who owned the garden where she lived was very old but his main joy in life was to care for his roses. His one dream in life was to breed a rose that was not only the most beautiful but also the one that would be loved by millions of people - from the ordinary working man or woman to the king or queen of the land. He also wanted children to love his rose because he thought it important that children should care for flowers as much as their toys.

A slow plodding could be heard coming down the garden path - every so often it would stop and someone would murmur. A cheeky robin merrily whistled as a blackbird and missel thrush vied with each other to greet the beautiful day with reams of glorious song. They did not falter as the person walking towards them, the old man who owned the garden, approached. They knew him as a friend as he had tenderly cared for them throughout the cold winter. In fact, they had got to know him so well that when it had been a particularly cold spell, it was not unknown for them all to perch on top of an old grandfather clock in the sitting room.

The old man's name was James Green, but all his friends called him Jim. He was liked by everyone in the village and was also highly respected as a fine gardener. Not as spry as he used to be, he could still be relied upon to give advice to anyone seeking information about gardening matters. Gradually he made his way to the sheltered spot where his beloved rose bush stood. He stopped now and then to gently straighten the odd bloom here and there or, with a 'Tut' of irritation, pluck a small weed out of the soil. At last he reached the rose bush and stood back for a moment and gazed at what was to be the greatest achievement of his life. The warm, but not too hot, sun had done its work well. Before the delighted eyes of Jim Green was the most perfect rosebud to have bloomed.

It was the most delicate pink and the edge of each petal was tinged all the way round by a deeper shade of pink, while up the centre of each petal, was one single line in the same darker colour. Tenderly Jim cupped the little rosebud in his gnarled old hand and breathed, 'Now aren't you a real beauty, my dear!' Tears formed in his eyes as he gazed proudly at the rose bush, for what he saw now was the result of many, many years of plotting, planning, care and hard work, and, most of all, keeping a great secret.

Eighteen years ago the king had been blessed with the birth of a beautiful daughter and he had told his chancellor that when she came of age on her eighteenth birthday, he wanted a rose to be especially created for her. Because he was a good and kind man, he wanted every one of his subjects who were interested in breeding roses, to be given the opportunity to offer a new rose for the occasion. - no matter if they did so professionally or as a hobby. Jim Green had been told of this venture by another gardener who specialised in vegetables, but who often sat long hours talking to Jim about all sorts of gardening matters.

Several weeks passed until one day Jim was up extremely early and, accompanied by his dawn chorus of robin, blackbird and missel thrush, was raking the path as he made his way to the rose bush where the little rosebud was now kept company by dozens more rosebuds - none yet as magnificent as her.

'You've got to stay as straight and as lovely as ever, my beauty,' said Jim, 'we've company today, important company too!' He gently straightened the little rosebud and then turned back up to the cottage.

Two hours later, a murmur of voices could be heard as they approached the rose bush. The three birds were singing so hard that one deep voice said, 'I must say that those birds sing better than any I've heard in many a long day. You obviously care for them or they'd not sing like that.'

'Yes, Sir,' replied Jim Green, 'I do care for them. They bring me such joy in the dark days of winter and they make sure my garden is a happy one.' After such a long speech, old Jim looked quite embarrassed.

At last three men stood before the rose bush. One man, the one who had spoken to Jim earlier, stepped forward whilst the other two stood back respectfully. The one in front gazed at the little rosebud and then, as gently as old Jim, cupped the beautiful bloom in his hand. After a few minutes, he turned to Jim and said, 'My dear man, never have I seen such a magnificent rose - I assure you that I will look no further for the rose I seek.' Turning to the other man, who was in fact his head gardener, he said, 'Frensham, what do you think?'

Frensham stepped up to the man and said, 'Your Majesty, I do indeed agree with you. Mr Green has bred the finest rose I have ever had the pleasure of looking at. What's more, Sire, it is a strong rose too, with a good straight stem. He is to be congratulated!'

Jim Green's face was a picture as his king beckoned him forward. 'Let it be known Jim Green, throughout the realm, that you have created the finest rose in the land. This rose will be the one chosen for my dear daughter's coming of age and I want you to present her with the bloom I have just seen, two days from now. As for the name - what could be more fitting than 'King's Joy'.'

A MONKEY'S TALE
G E Harrison

Widawish was a monkey who lived with his family in Mudawunkey Land. They all lived together very happily in their own monkey house, which had wonderful views of the sea and the beach. Enormous palm trees could be seen everywhere. Behind their house there was a huge forest where Widawish and his brothers and sisters liked to play! They had so much fun! From dawn until bedtime they would play, until Mummy Monkey would have to go outside into the forest to find them all!

Widawish was a naughty monkey! He was always disappearing and Mummy Monkey used to be so worried. Then, when Widawish returned home, he would hide, as he would be worried about what Mummy Monkey would do. Usually she was simply relieved to have Widawish home safely!

Most days were happy and Widawish went to the local Monkey School with all the other monkeys in the neighbourhood. They all went to school on the school bus which stopped outside every monkey house. All the monkeys had their own school bags to carry school books, sports gear and their lunch boxes. Every monkey would be waiting outside their own monkey houses watching for the school bus to arrive. Widawish was always on time for the school bus and his best friend, Wudawant, always saved a seat for Widawish, as he was on the school bus first.

Eventually, when all the monkeys were safely on the school bus, the monkey driver, Mr Chiddawink, would say 'All aboard! And off we go!'

They would eventually arrive at school and they would all get off the school bus and would have to form an orderly line. The head monkey teacher, Mrs Headamonk, used to be very cross sometimes, just because they did not always want to form an orderly line!

Some of the young monkeys would be talking so quietly, but one of the prefects from the perfectmunk team would sometimes hear them and that could only mean one thing, trouble.

'Widawish, come out of the queue now!'

Then, the long walk to Mrs Headamonk's office. Widawish would be so scared; he just wanted to go home to see Mummy Monkey. He knew he had to take his punishment like a 'grown up' monkey, but he was only a little monkey! He told Mrs Headamonk he was very sorry for talking, when he knew it was not allowed, but he was told he would have to stay after school for fifteen minutes! Widawish was very upset! It would mean that he would miss the school bus home and he would not see Mr Chiddawink, the monkey driver. It would also mean that his parents would find out that he had been a naughty little monkey. If only he had not asked his monkey friend for some of his banana! Widawish would eat all his breakfast every day, after all the trouble he had caused for himself!

Widawish went to his classroom and sat on his chair quietly, tucking his back legs and his long tail under his body. His friend, Wudawant, wondered why he was so quiet. He realised Widawish must have been punished by Mrs Headamonk, the head teacher, when Widawish had been late coming into class, looking so sad. Wudawant would have to cheer him up at break-time.

As the morning went on, Widawish began to feel much better. He was able to answer some of the teacher's questions and the teacher was giving him some well deserved praise. Eventually it was break-time and Widawish could hardly wait to leave, but he was very careful not to talk!

Wudawant went to play with Widawish, and they ran around the playground shrieking their heads off! They saw their teacher, Mrs Kiddawink, coming across the playground and, to avoid any further trouble, Widawish shouted to Wudawant, 'Quickly, run up this tree and then we can hide!' They both made a run for the tree and managed to climb fast enough and far enough into the tree, so that they could not be seen! Once they felt safe, they ran upwards, through the branches of the tree, and arrived at the climbing frame centre. They both longed to be able to spend a whole day in that place. They both knew that, when they heard the school bell ringing, they would have to run very fast to be in their classroom in time for their next lesson. Wudawant did not run as fast as Widawish, so Widawish said to Wudawant, 'We'll have to really hurry! If you are having any problems, I'll let you ride on my back all the way to the classroom. In fact, if you do that, we can have a few more minutes here!'

So, Wudawant had to think quickly because he did not have much time. He decided that Widawish was truly his very best friend! When they heard the bell ringing, Widawish shouted, 'Come on Wudawant.'

Wudawant ran as fast as he could and jumped onto Widawish's back and Widawish shouted, 'Hold on as hard as you can, but try not to choke me!'

Wudawant did just as Widawish has asked him and held on, trying not to choke Widawish. Unfortunately Widawish had not realised Wudawant was so heavy! They would be late for class if Widawish had to stop to have a rest. They managed to travel across the playground and could see the entrance to their classroom when suddenly Wudawant sneezed! Widawish got such a fright! He stumbled forwards and Wudawant was still holding onto Widawish and was screaming his head off!

They heard someone shouting, 'Just what do you two monkeys think you are doing? Why aren't you in class?'

Oh no! The voice was that of Mrs Headamonk! They were in big trouble again!

They were both on the ground and Wudawant was still holding onto Widawish who was having difficulty breathing. 'Get off me, get off my back right now. You are too heavy for me.'

Mrs Headamonk roared at both of them, 'Get up at once! What on earth are you doing? Go to my office immediately! Do you hear me?'

Widawish was fighting back his tears and was trying to stand up as fast as he could, but he was feeling uncomfortable after their tumble. Wudawant was crying and Widawish was trying to comfort him when Mrs Headamonk shouted, 'If you don't stop crying I'll be really cross!'

Wudawant, with a struggle, managed to stop crying and simply sniffled.

Now we are definitely for it! Widawish had thought. He was really worried. That was the second time he had been in trouble in the same day and it wasn't even lunchtime! Well, he had only hoped that whatever Mrs Headamonk was going to say would not take very long, or both Wudawant and himself would miss attendance for their next class. Mrs Headamonk told them that she did not want to see either of them behaving in such an unsafe and irresponsible way again. Did they not realise how dangerous their actions had been? Did they never stop to think that they might have had an accident? As it was they had stumbled and she asked if they were all right.

Widawish had said, 'We are very sorry, aren't we, Wudawant? We will not do anything like that again, Mrs Headamonk. Please may we go to our class now?

Wudawant was very quiet. He simply wanted to leave Mrs Headamonk's office as quickly as possible. Mrs Headamonk dismissed them both, but not without warning, 'Any more stunts like this one and I shall have no option but to inform your parents. Do you understand?'

Both Widawish and Wudawant nodded their heads showing Mrs Headamonk that they had understood. They were too worried to speak in case they said something wrong and would be in more trouble!' Mrs Headamonk dismissed them and they managed to make their way to their classroom despite the fact that they were both feeling rather sore following their fall! They would not be in a hurry to do that again!

Widawish sensed an overwhelming desire to escape into his own little world of imagination! When Widawish felt that nothing was going right for him and that every single thing he did was resulting in trouble for himself, the only way to escape was to imagine he was somewhere else!

On this particular day, Widawish was so desperate to escape that he soon began to lose his concentration in class and hopefully the teacher, Mrs Kidderwink, would not notice his faraway gaze!

Widawish imagined he was going on a long journey, far away from school, and away from trouble! He was alone on his journey, having left his friend, Wudawant behind. Widawish, in his imaginary journey, left school and travelled on the local monkey bus to the railway station, a journey in his real world that he would never make alone. That was what made everything so exciting! Widawish asked the stationmaster, Mr Nadderwite, what time the train left the station to travel to the space shuttle. The next train was due to leave in six minutes! Widawish just had time to visit the shop on the station platform to buy some refreshments for the journey. He hoped he would have enough money! He bought a bottle of water to drink, an apple, a banana and a small bar of chocolate. When Widawish arrived at the checkout, the salesperson put his purchases in a small carrier bag. Widawish paid for his chosen items! *What a relief to have had enough money,* Widawish had thought.

He heard the train approaching! He had known that it was the train to the space shuttle station because the monkey stationmaster, Mr Nadderwite, had told him which platform he needed to be on. Widawish was so excited! The train slowly approached and then stopped. The passengers got off the train and the ongoing passengers waited on the platform to board the train and, within a few minutes, were allowed to do so. Widawish managed to find a window seat, as he always like to be able to look out of the window. The stationmaster blew his whistle and he was on his way! It was simply great! At first the train moved slowly but, once the railway station was out of sight, Widawish was aware that the train was travelling at very high speed! He was wanting to arrive at the destination, but would have to be patient. It was quite a long journey, well, for a little monkey like himself! He was able to see out of the window until it began to rain very hard and then he could not see very much at all. This seemed to make the journey so much longer! Widawish was thinking about his friend, Wudawant, and was missing his company! The ticket inspector asked him for his ticket. Thankfully his ticket was in order!

Widawish was looking at his watch and realised that the train would soon be arriving at the station and that he would soon be on his way to board the space shuttle! He could hardly wait! He began to become very restless and was fidgeting. The lady sitting opposite him looked at Widawish with a very stern expression on her face. Just at that moment, he heard a very familiar voice in his ear, 'Widawish, are you still with us or somewhere else? Now Widawish, tell me where we are in our class work please.'

It was the voice of his teacher, Mrs Kidderwink! Widawish could not answer and Mrs Kidderwink ordered him to remain after school in detention! Widawish was so fed up!

So, as he was already in trouble, Widawish thought he could not possibly be in any worse trouble if he returned to his imaginary journey! So, within minutes of being in trouble with Mrs Kidderwink, Widawish had arrived at his destination at the railway station, where he would leave the train to join the space shuttle!

Widawish left the train and followed the signs to the space shuttle terminal with the other passengers. He boarded the moon buggy and, once seated, made sure his seat belt was secure. The moon buggy travelled at very high speed! Once all the passengers were secure and their seat belts had been checked by the space hostess, they were off to join the space shuttle! The track was very bumpy and littered with debris from outer space, which made the journey very exciting! After about fifteen minutes, the moon buggy arrived at the space shuttle! The excitement was exhilarating! After disembarking, Widawish had to enter a capsule to collect his spacesuit, protective helmet and space shoes. He felt very comfortable and everything fitted him! He was ready!

Then the voice of Mrs Kidderwink sounding in his ear brought Widawish back to Earth with a shock! Would he ever be able to go on his imaginary journey again?

THE SHORT-SIGHTED ELEPHANT
Audrey Luckhurst

Rix was a short-sighted elephant and when he was young his mother used her trunk to guide him along. When male elephants are grown up they have to leave the herd and take care of themselves; when this happened the male elephant stayed together in small groups. Sadly for Rix, none of them wanted him in their group as he was always bumping into them. He felt very sad and lonely.

Chapter 2

In a tiny hole under a bush Dell, a tiny mouse, shook with fear; when he was small his mother often got cross with him because he was so timid.

'Dell,' she would say, 'you really mist try and overcome your fears. However will you be able to hunt in the forest for your food when you are grown up?'

Well he was grown up now and he was hungry. In spite of being nervous he would have to go hunting for food. First he poked his nose out of the hole and sniffed the air, then he popped his head out far enough to see if there were any dangers he would have to overcome. Slowly he moved his whole body out of the hole. He had only taken a few steps when he spied a large elephant sleeping on the ground nearby.

Chapter 3

The snapping of a twig made Dell look sideways; it was a wild cat sneaking up on him. Quick as a flash he dived under a flap of the elephant's ears to hide. The cat pounced and landed on the elephant's ear and its sharp claws dug into it. Rix, whose ear it was, howled with pain and lashed out with his trunk and hit the offending cat on the backside which sent it scampering away. Dell, fearful lest the elephant was cross with him too, trembled as he cringed inside the elephant's ear and said, 'Please don't be cross with me; I was afraid the cat would catch and eat me so I ran under your ear flap and hid in your ear. Can I go now?'

'Tell me something of yourself first, I could do with someone to talk to me as I get very lonely.'

Chapter 4

Rix and Dell spent most of the day together; they enjoyed each other's company, they talked about their problems and worked out a solution beneficial to them both. Dell would ride on Rix's back, that way he would be safe from the wild cats and he could act as Rix's eyes and prevent him from bumping into the other elephants.

Chapter 5

The place where Rix and Dell lived was deep in a large forest. Only animals and insects resided there. Neither had ever seen a human being or had ever heard of one so it was a bit strange when they saw an odd looking creature float down from the sky and land in a tree.

Fiona Fayburn grasped a branch of the tree with one hand as she struggled to free herself from her parachute with the other. Glancing downwards she became aware of two pairs of eyes watching her. One pair, though small, had a wide open penetrating gaze, the other pair were screwed up as if they had difficulty seeing what was taking place in front of them. She freed herself from most of her tangled parachute but was unable to reach one piece of cord holding her trapped and helpless.

Fiona, dangling in the tree, disturbed a group of monkeys in nearby trees. They plucked hard unripe fruit and, screeching loudly, threw them at her.

Rix, who had perfect hearing, hated the noise; filling his trunk with water from a nearby stream, he squirted the monkeys with it. The monkeys didn't like getting wet so they ran away.

Chapter 6

Rix and Dell discussed the creature dangling in the tree.

'It's trapped and can't get down. Shall we help it?'

'Do you think it's dangerous, Dell?'

Surprisingly Dell, who was usually so fearful, said, 'Let's find out. If you stretch your trunk upwards towards the tree I'll climb up and gnaw through the cord binding it to the tree.'

This Rix did. He couldn't quite reach so he rested his front legs on a low branch and stretched out far enough for Dell to scamper up and bite through the offending cord. As the cord parted Dell was left dangling at the end of one of the pieces. Fiona, afraid for her rescuer's safety, reached out and lifted him onto her shoulder, then climbed down from the tree. It felt good to be on firm ground but this feeling didn't last long as a large trunk curled around her waist and she was lifted high onto the elephant's back.

Chapter 7

Uncertain of what would happen next, Fiona remembered she still had her backpack strapped to her shoulders. In it were three sandwiches; she took them out and shared them with her rescuers as a sign of her appreciation. The elephant quickly devoured his; the little mouse nibbled a little of his and the elephant ate the remainder. Fiona spent the rest of the day with her rescuers and that night curled up beside them until the first light of dawn appeared.

The first thing Rix did on waking was to bathe in the nearby stream; he took Fiona by surprise when he showered her and the little mouse with water. It became obvious to her this was a normal routine for them, one they both seemed to enjoy. Cold water showers weren't exactly what she was used to. Without a towel to dry herself or her clothes she felt most uncomfortable; the best she could do was hang her clothes over the branch of a nearby tree and cover herself with large leaves plucked from a bush. Dell thought her actions were odd; he never removed his fur and always rolled in dry grass after his shower.

In companionable silence the three spent the morning foraging for food. Fiona was delighted at the variety of ripe fruit there was to eat. When they had eaten their fill they rested for a while. Fiona thought about finding a way out of the forest. Maybe the best way would be to follow the stream, but did it go deeper into the forest? She searched her pack to see if she still had her compass, it wasn't there. Many of the trees were very tall. If she could climb to the top of one of them she would be able to get a clearer view of her surroundings.

Chapter 8

Fiona heard the sound of an aircraft flying low above the trees; was it an aircraft searching for her - if only she could send up a signal? Even as the thought flashed into her head, she heard a noise as if something had fallen on the ground; it was a survival kit. Before she had time to open it, Rix and Dell, full of curiosity, arrived on the scene. They sniffed around it, but soon lost interest because it was non-edible. Eagerly Fiona opened the package. Among other things it contained a torch; now she would be able to flash a signal when she next heard the plane flying above. The package also contained a small camera with film. She decided to take a photograph of her new friends. In fact she took several; they seemed puzzled by her actions, but at the same time they enjoyed the attention she was giving them.

Chapter 9

It was in the evening when she heard a plane flying overhead. She quickly used the torch to flash a message in code; a message was flashed back that a rescue helicopter would pick her up the following morning at first light.

She looked forward to going home but was sad to be leaving her friends so soon after meeting them; she had grown very fond of the unusual pair.

Early the next morning, wishing to avoid getting a shower, she rose before her two friends and prepared for the arrival of the helicopter. The second she heard it flying overhead she stood in a small clearing and flashed her torch to let the pilot know exactly where she was. Aware that her friends were now awake and watching her, she gave each one of them a friendly pat. As if sensing she was leaving them, Rix gently patted her cheek with his trunk and Dell jumped onto her shoulder and tickled her nose with his whiskers.

The helicopter's winch was let down. Fiona fastened herself in, giving Rix and Dell a last wave, she was hauled up into the helicopter.

Rix and Dell often spoke of the strange creature who had floated down from the sky and how a big flying spider had let down a long web then pulled it up an eaten it.

Fiona wrote of her adventure, added the photographs of her animal friends. It became a big success story enjoyed by many readers.

RICARDO: THE ONION MAN AND HIS BICYCLE
Gerard Allardyce

It was Ricardo's eightieth birthday and he was making his last trip to England selling his onions. He was full of sadness despite the warm, sunny weather. There were no more onion men. He was the last of a splendid generation of generations that had sold onions to the English since the early twenties of the twentieth century. Some of these onion men had been very poor, old soldiers eager to make a living. He, Ricardo, had seen them all. He looked out onto the piece of water that separated France from England and became deep in thought, enjoying the occasional swig from a wine bottle. The red wine made him feel good. Then he could see the cliffs of Dover.

The next day Ricardo arrived at about four in the afternoon in the quaint little town of Horsham after a very hard ride. Such was the nature of his bike and packing that he had nearly run out of a neck of onions. He came to a little semi-detached house and knocked on the door in a friendly manner. A little boy answered the door.

'Good afternoon. My name is Ricardo and please may I ask your name?'

'Jamie,' the little boy replied.

'Can I speak to your mummy?'

'I'll call Mummy . . . Mummy,' the boy shouted inside the house. 'There is a strange man outside the door.'

The mother came to the door and Ricardo was pleasantly surprised by what he could see of Jamie's mother. He saw a lady who was beautiful and very shapely, and who reminded him with her auburn hair of his dear late wife who had died in the war.

'My word Madame, your little boy has a mouth just like his mother,' and with that Jamie's mum laughed with merriment. 'Oh dear Madame, I didn't mean to sound like that.' And with that they both laughed like drains.

'My little boy told me your name was Ricardo. My name is Elena and I am pleased to meet you.'

'I am an onion man Elena, the last onion man and very, very old.'

'Have you always been an onion man Ricardo?'

'No Jamie, I have been a chef on the Orient Express before the war and then a member of the resistance movement fighting the Germans.

Oh, I forgot Jamie, you do not know much about things like war, resistance movement or anything of that nature. How old are you?'

'I am six. I am a big boy.'

'You are a big boy Jamie,' his mother said, patting him on the head and he looked up smiling. Then she addressed the very tall onion man with his cravat and long white trench coat. 'If you are French, why do you have an Italian Christian name, why are you called Ricardo?'

'I am called Ricardo because my mother is Italian. My father happens to be French and we lived in Caen in the province of Normandy. I live in the little fishing village of Arcachon.'

'Oh I know Ricardo. Arcachon is near Cap Ferrett. Patrick, my husband, had an aunt that lived in Cap Ferrett throughout the war. She left Paris just before the Germans captured it and lived in Cap Ferrett. There she was safe.' There was no more talking for the moment until Elena referred to Ricardo's mother.

'My mother's name was Maria and do you now something Elena, she was the spitting image of her namesake Maria Callas. And I've heard my mother sing like her and bring the house down in the town theatre in Caen.'

'That's amazing Ricardo . . . to have a mother to sing and share the great same name of Maria Callas.'

Ricardo suddenly took a net full of onions from around his neck and gave them to Elena.

'Thank you Ricardo. How much do I owe you for them?'

'Nothing my lady. As I am the last onion man to come to England and you are my last house, I give you them for free.'

'That's very kind of you Ricardo.'

'Mummy, we can use the onions for a stew.'

'That's a very good idea Jamie.'

'Oh thank you Ricardo. Jamie is into cookery.'

There was an intent look on the onion man's face. Jamie suddenly spoke. 'Why do your country hate us Ricardo?'

'Jamie, Jamie, Jamie, France likes England. Everyone likes each other now, including Germany.'

'Jamie gets upset when he sees the entente cordialle not working Ricardo.'

Suddenly Ricardo said something which made Jamie and his mother listen carefully. 'Jamie, would you like a ride on my magic bicycle?'

'Oh yes please Ricardo,' Jamie replied.

'Mummy, can I ride on Ricardo's magic bicycle?'

'Of course you can Jamie.' Then as an aside, 'How long will you both be gone Ricardo?'

'Only about twenty-five minutes Madame, exactement.'

Little Jamie only left the house and his mummy to go to school and although he liked Ricardo, it was like anyone else, he was a little worried like when he spent the afternoon with Daddy he missed Mummy and when he was back at home with Mummy, he missed Daddy. The sad fact was that Jamie came from a broken home. He was a happy little boy who could not really understand why his mummy and daddy lived apart.

'Elena,' Ricardo spoke softly clutching his ancient trusty steed, his bicycle, 'I shall bring you back the most excellent of red wine from France namely Chateau Nuit St Georges 1945.'

Elena answered Ricardo as if cut off from this world she was living in but fully conscious of the import of what he had said. Her voice betrayed a certain emotion. She had red eyes and was about to cry. 'My grandad was a captain in the army Ricardo. He fought his way from the Normandy beaches to Berlin. He was Ricardo, an officer with Lord Lovat's regiment.'

'Fantastic soldiers all of them Elena and I have proved so often that the old relationship of peace, love and friendship between France and Great Britain is very much alive.'

'Do you know Ricardo, when my grandfather died of cancer nearly twenty years ago, my father had a very emotional piece of music played at the crematorium namely 'All Over The World There Are People In Love' by an excellent French singer called Francois Hardy.'

The sun had died down as Ricardo looked gently into Elena's eyes. Although he was nearly eighty-one, he had the bearing and vigour of a twenty-one year old and he answered Elena sympathetically and with a knowing smile only a Frenchman could conjure up, 'I too like that song of Francois Hardy but now Madame I must take Jamie on his little bike ride. Jamie, do you know the word for bicycle in French?'

'Of course Ricardo, bicyclette.'

'Bon. Say goodbye to your loving mother and we will go.'

'Bye bye Mummy.'

Jamie sat on a cushion in the front pannier and soon the old bike was soaring over the rooftops leaving Jamie's little house far away.

'I fly a bicycle the same way as I used to fly a broomstick many years ago Jamie.'

'Are you Wizard Ricardo?'

'Sort of . . . I learnt how to cast spells and fly broomsticks when I was a boy and gave up at the age of eighteen. I was a rebel in the family Jamie.'

'What does that mean Ricardo?'

'Oh sorry, I am using complicated language. I didn't like it . . . '

'Oh I see. We are very high but I so like the ride.'

'The bicycle is more comfortable than a broomstick Jamie.'

It seemed a fleeting moment when they were gliding over Horsham Park, the RC Church of St John the Evangelist and the wonderful little museum.

'My father, Jamie, was an airman in the First World War. He picked up a nice little song from an English pilot.'

'Do sing the little old song Ricardo.'

'Well Jamie, it went like this . . .

They all looked up and said it is a fairy,

A cockledoodledoo or a canary?

When I fly in the sky they all shout as I pass by,

Airman, airman,

Don't put the wind up me . . .

And, Jamie, there is a second little verse as we fly over the sea to France.

They all looked up and said is it a fairy,

A cockledoddledo or a canary?

When I fly they all shout as I pass by,

Airman, airman,

Don't put the wind up me.

And Jamie don't put the linnet out.'

The little boy was so happy flying with Ricardo, on the onion man's bike.

'Are we going to France Ricardo?'

'Yes we are. For a little boy you are very clever.'

Soon they were flying over the French coast and in Paris.

'Are we landing soon Ricardo?'

'Yes,' the wizard said with intent in his voice. 'We are going to see your great grandfather, Captain Hazelwood, at the Majestic Hotel. We have gone into a time zone, all of my own making. It is 1945 and we will, in just a second, be joining your great grandfather at a table in the boulevard outside the hotel.'

Just before they arrived at the Hotel Majestic, Jamie could hear the voice of Francois Hardy and the words of her emotional song, 'All Over The World People Are Falling In Love'.

'Good evening Captain, my name is Ricardo and I am going to introduce you to your great grandson, and do you not think he looks like you?'

'My great grandson, Elena's boy . . . hello son.'

'Hello Great Grandad.'

Jamie sidled up to the war hero who was wearing his military cross . . .

Ricardo spoke softly as usual. There was a spiritual quality in his voice. 'How are you finding the French people Captain?'

'They are so friendly, wonderful people. They love us for liberating their country and in turn, we love them.'

'Quite Captain,' Ricardo replied. 'It is only the politicians who sow the feeling of hate between the two nations.'

'Thank you for coming here Ricardo with my great grandson. Here is a bottle of Nuit St Georges 1945 vintage, and for you Jamie, a fistful of French francs.'

Soon all Jamie and Ricardo could see was the silhouettes of people and the oncoming of night.

Jamie was in a heavy sleep on a Saturday morning when his mother woke him up.

'Where's the onion man Mummy?'

'What onion man Jamie?'

'I saw Great Grandad . . . '

'Now, now, now Jamie, you are just dreaming. Here is a glass of warm milk for you to drink,' and with that Elena went downstairs to do some housework.

For some reason Jamie lifted his pillow and there underneath was his great grandfather's military cross and ribbon. With joy in his heart he went to his little bedroom window and looked outside onto a blue sky and shining sun.

'You are somewhere in the sky Great Grandad, I know you are. Come back onion man.'

EVEN A STAR'S WISHES COME TRUE
Patricia Green

Chapter 1 - The Lonely Star

If you look up at the sky on a winter's night you will see one lonely star. This lonely star is watching over you when you are asleep. If you look carefully you will see the lonely star has a smile - a sad smile.

One day the lonely star was given a name, 'Lucky Star'. I will take you on an exciting journey, there you will be able to see why the star got its name.

The day started off with the birds singing way up high in the treetops as the sun was coming up to shine brightly. There wasn't a cloud in the sky. Lucky Star was just going to asleep when *bang! What was that?* thought Lucky Star.

With his sleepy eyes he couldn't make out where it was coming from, then there was a big flash, so bright for a minute the star was blinded. The star didn't panic but instead was overcome by surprise.

In the distance the star had seen the big flash and heard the loud bang. The star wondered what it was, but he didn't have to wait long to find out. The star then yawned and went back to sleep, thinking of what would be in store for him the next night.

As soon as he nodded off things began to happen. A small, twinkling light was moving forward, towards where the star was sleeping. As it got nearer it began to make a shape just like the sleeping star. The nearer it came the more it shone. This woke up the sleeping star and he shouted out, 'I must be dreaming!' But no, he wasn't, there before him was the most beautiful sight he ever saw. He would no longer be alone for he had found a friend. That's why and how he got his name, 'Lucky Star'.

Chapter 2 - My New Friend And I

The two stars were getting on well together. Lucky Star soon thought of a name to call his friend, but I will tell you that later. Now the next journey is to find out if the new star is a boy or girl, but Lucky Star didn't care, he had a friend.

The nights went by when they would both shine in the dark sky. The two stars were very happy. Lucky Star wasn't much older than his new friend, but that didn't matter.

One night Lucky Star noticed that his friend hadn't grown anymore. He thought this rather odd. He didn't say anything to his friend, Lucky Star just thought for a while. Looking at his small friend, the star had a job to do. He knew he had to look after his friend, so that is what he did; that is what friends are for.

Lucky Star felt so good about himself and he named his friend 'Bright Star'. Over the next few years they will learn about themselves, but that's another story. For now we have two good friends - Lucky Star and Bright Star, together in the sky.

Chapter 3 - Bright Star Disappears

Everything was going right. Lucky Star and Bright Star were in their happy moods, but one day Bright Star disappeared. This is how the story goes.

Every day Bright Star kept having bad dreams. In her dreams she saw another star, but this star wasn't a good star. She knew that it wasn't her friend Lucky Star. These dreams began to worry her. Lucky Star started to notice something was wrong with her Bright Star, but being Lucky Star he was well in thought, that was what he was used to. Lucky Star didn't do anything until he was quite sure it was the right thing to do for his friend Bright Star. He wouldn't hurt his friend, not if he could help it. Anyway, Lucky Star thought no more of it. While they were sleeping Bright Star was drifting further away from Lucky Star. When Bright Star woke up she found herself alone. Lucky Star was nowhere to be seen. Her first thought was that she couldn't make out where he had gone. She knew Lucky Star wouldn't leave her for long as they were still good friends. One star didn't think bad of the other star.

By this time Lucky Star had woken. He thought the worst so he went in search for his friend Bright Star. All he had to do was look for a bright light as they were the only two stars in the sky, but it wasn't that easy, *he could go on forever,* he thought.

By this time Bright Star was as big as she could get. One night, as the moon was out, something magical happened. Bright Star has made a lot of small stars which lit up the whole sky. Lucky Star was always in the right place again. He was awoken with a *bang!* The baby stars made their way towards him. Bright Star shone even brighter.

Lucky Star thought he was dreaming, but you know, if you follow a star your dreams could come true, just like Lucky's had.

They all lived happily ever after. If you look into the sky you will see them. Make a wish and climb back into your bed. Close your eyes and think of me.

THE TOURNAMENT
J Millington

Within the castle walls everything was a-buzz. A bird flying by would be forgiven for thinking it was flying over a town because it *was* a king of a town. Every craft and industry was carried on.

There were forges for the making of armour, swords, tools, horse harnesses, horse shoes and even ploughs for farming; tanneries where Hide was prepared for the making of leather goods. Craftsmen were making jewellery, pins for fastening clothing, buckles and gold and silver goblets. Others were weaving cloth to be made into garments. People were filling the granaries with corn, others weaving every kind of basket. Butchers were sending carcasses to the coolest places in the castle. Huge vats were filled with fat which was to be made into candles and rush lights. Barrels of wine were trundled over the drawbridge to be stored too, in cool places. Bakers were baking bread - a wonderful aroma on the morning air! Knights were practising ready for the jousts. The sun glinted on their armour.

Hundreds of people lived within the castle walls. Padima was one of those people, but her father, the earl, owned the castle.

Everyone said she was beautiful and she was so sweet but it didn't spoil her.

She was rather sad because her parents thought it was time she got married and she didn't want to because she didn't love anyone.

Her parents wanted her to choose between three handsome knights, Sir Wenlock, Sir Mortimer or Sir Conrad. She couldn't choose because she liked them all as brothers.

The earl thought that as she couldn't make up her mind, he'd arrange a tournament and said that whichever of the three knights won, they would have her hand in marriage.

Truth to tell, the three knights didn't want to marry Padima either. They loved *her* as a sister and also they all had their eyes already on the girls they wanted to marry, but they knew their lives would be in peril if they disobeyed the earl, so, heavy hearted, they practised every day for the tournament.

Sometimes the earl looked on and was pleased at what he saw. The three knights were certainly good. Whichever one won, the earl knew his daughter would have a good husband. Nodding, he was well satisfied with them.

When their spell of duty was over, the knights could go to their own homes. Each of their families had their own land and Sir Wenlock loved to help farm the land. Happiness to him meant watching a golden cornfield sway to and fro in a stiff breeze. It meant the land had been tilled, seeds down, green shoots pushing up through the earth and then the golden corn living through spring, summer and to autumn. It gave him a very satisfied feeling.

Sir Mortimer leaned towards the clergy. Had he not been a knight he'd have become a parson. He was a good man and read his bible every day. He knew it by heart. However, he was by no means dull.

Sir Conrad was the huntin', shootin', fishing type. He rode his horse for miles around his folks' estate. He was a complete open-air man. He was a compassionate man though and people on the estate adored him.

As the day of the very special jousts came ever nearer, people from far and wide arrived at the castle, to witness the event, among them jesters and dancing bears.

Padima watched all the bustle with rather a heavy heart. Then she became aware of a beautiful voice singing. It lifted her heart. When the singing stopped she sent a man to find the singer and bring him to her.

Nick, the minstrel, had come a long way and felt tired, but before finding somewhere to sleep for the night, and with all the crowd, where was he likely to find anywhere? He would sing one song. It was a plaintive melody which he sang beneath the castle walls. Padima heard it.

The man she sent out soon found Nick. He had his lyre slung round his neck.

Taking him to Padima, the man turned and left. Lifting his eyes to Padima he fell in love with what he saw and she fell in love with him - they both fell in love at once with each other.

What could Padima do? Her father, she was sure, would not stop the tournament, nor would he accept the idea of her marrying a minstrel, that was if the minstrel wanted to marry *her*. Looking into his eyes, she had not doubt of that.

Padima had never seen a more beautiful man than Nick. His hair waved and curled and his eyes danced. She was enchanted. Nick felt the same about Padima. She was a goddess, but how could he hope to win her. His heart sank. So, while he thought, he softly played his lyre. Padima sat and listened. Looking behind Nick, Padima saw her father, the earl, at the open door. Amazed, she saw that he was listening to Nick's music. Softly, he came nearer. He never attempted to stop his musician.

Nick's hand fell from the instrument to his side and his head fell forward. Making his straighten up suddenly, the earl shouted, 'Bravo! Bravo! A fine sound young man, come and play for me while we have our meal.'

Bowing to Padima, Nick followed the earl. His tiredness was now forgotten. He knew the earl would get him a bed for the night. Also, he would be near Padima. Oh yes, he knew her name because everyone knew the three knights were vying for her hand.

Later on Padima saw Nick and heard his beautiful playing and singing. He charmed her father as no other musician had ever done.

The earl insisted he stay at the castle as his own troubadour. Nick didn't need asking twice, although he still hadn't the faintest idea how he could ever claim Padima. And she? She also racked her brains for a way to bring her father round to the idea of having Nick as his son-in-law. And all the while Nick's music was winding its way into the earl's heart.

Up to now Padima thought he hadn't noticed Nick - only his voice and his music - so a few days before the tournament she told her father she didn't want any of the three knights as a husband, as she loved Nick.

The earl thought she was mad and refused to listen anymore. Poor Padima wept for hours.

Her talk with the earl made that man really see Nick though. He liked what he saw - but as his daughter's husband? No!

Next time Nick played and sang for him, the earl couldn't help seeing him as a person in his own right. However, Padima would marry the winner in the jousts.

The day came at last. It was a beautiful morning. The sun poured into Padima's room, wakening her. Her heart felt leaden. Then under her window she heard the sweetest, saddest song she had ever heard in her life. Nick was singing for her alone.

Throwing a cloak over her shoulders she ran down the steps to where Nick was singing. When he saw her he stopped. She ran into his arms sobbing. She asked him to run away with her there and then, but Nick knew it would be foolish to do so, as he had no money for them to live on, but Padima pleaded so that at last he said that they would run away after the tournament, as all those people had come to the castle to enjoy themselves and would be angry if that enjoyment was spoiled by their elopement.

Padima at last saw that Nick was right. She must endure the next few hours. Getting another promise from Nick that he would be waiting for her, she turned and went back to her room.

Later on she sat in the midst of the lively crowd with her parents.

For some days the earl had been thinking about Nick. The boy's playing and singing soothed and placated him more than he would ever have thought possible and somehow he sensed that if he could not marry Padima, Nick would go. He didn't want that.

However, his attention was caught by the action going on in front of him. Oh, Sir Conrad was down. That was the first contender out.

In between jousts the spectators watched conjurors, jugglers, tumblers, dancing bears and all kinds of amusements. They also bought pies and sweetmeats from the men who carried trays of them on their heads.

Nick bought a posy for Padima from a flower girl. When he sang and played his music people threw money at his feet.

Padima's heart turned over every time she looked at him. In her room she'd put everything ready for when he came for her; her clothes, money, jewellery and also some food and wine.

Sir Mortimer was showing his paces. Ah, he was off. Second contestant gone. There was only Sir Wenlock left. If he lost they would have to do the contest again.

Actually, Sir Conrad and Sir Mortimer had deliberately fallen off, although they knew that left the field clear for Sir Wenlock.

When Sir Wenlock saw what had happened he drew himself up and vowed that he would win Padima, because they were playing a dirty trick on her, none of them wanted to marry such a sweet girl.

When he was knocked off there was no one more surprised than himself! All three contestants were out.

Everyone expected the earl to call the three knights for another try, but instead he called Nick to his side.

Putting Padima's hand into the hand of Nick, the earl told the assembled crowd that the two would marry.

For a moment the happy couple were stunned, then they flew into each other's arms.

The three knights beamed and heaved sighs of relief. The earl told the merrymakers to continue.

Now he would be able to keep his musician and also his daughter, who were very happy.

HANNAH AND HER HEART
Kay Elizabeth

Hannah was a special little girl. There was only one small problem; she herself didn't think she was. Hannah wasn't really sure why she felt like that, just seemed to be something that she had always known . . . that she was nothing special.

She was small for her age, so she couldn't run as fast as the others that won the races. She was shy, so she found it hard to make friends and only had one (and some days none when her 'friend' didn't feel like being her friend that day). She didn't have beautiful, long blonde hair or lovely brown eyes like some of the other girls, nor was she outstanding in any of her classes. She was, she thought to herself, just, well . . . ordinary.

One night Hannah was lying in her soft, comfortable bed thinking about school tomorrow and the maths' test. She tossed and turned, finding it hard to sleep because, even though she always tried hard in class, she didn't know if she'd do well or not. She'd like to, just once, do better than average.

As she twiddled her stripy pyjama sleeves, gazing out at the night stars through her moonlit window, she heard something. Hannah frowned in the middle of a yawn, which is quite a funny face to see, not sure what the noise had been and stopping fidgeting. Yes, there it was again. Sounded like a whisper . . .

'Psst . . . Hannah,' said a small voice. Now, Hannah trembled a little at this unexpected event. Everyone else in the house was sleeping, she knew that. The voice wasn't scary though, she decided, it was soft and gentle, so her curiosity got the better of her.

'Yes? Hello? Who's that?' she asked, pulling her covers up just a bit more to her dimpled chin. Actually, it came out more like a squeak when she said it because she was still a little scared. Hannah squinted her eyes in the half light, trying to find the source of the voice.

'It's me! You don't know me?' said the voice, sounding surprised. 'Hannah, you and I go way back; all your life, actually!' A chuckle followed that statement.

Hannah screwed her face up in a puzzled look. 'Nope. Don't recognise the voice. Who are you?' she asked again, starting to sit up a bit now in bed, as she was feeling a bit braver.

'I'm your heart, Hannah,' said the voice.

'I didn't know hearts could talk!' Hannah exclaimed, sitting straight up now, eyes widening in her surprise.

'Oh yes Hannah, of course they can!' laughed her heart. 'It's just that sometimes you need to listen very carefully. But today I decided to shout instead of waiting to be listened to. Now then, Hannah,' said her heart, in a 'you're about to get a telling off' tone of voice, 'what's all this about you being ordinary? I can hear your thoughts you know, and I know you've been thinking about this a lot recently. Tell me about it.'

Hannah shifted uncomfortably in her bed, wondering if she was dreaming. She decided that if she was, it was a good dream anyway, so she might as well enjoy this strange conversation, since she didn't get the chance to talk much most of the time. 'Well . . . umm . . . I am . . . ' she trailed off sadly, realising it wasn't a great answer but hoping that her heart wouldn't notice.

'Uh huh . . . and why do you say that?' asked her heart, sounding to Hannah like it had indeed noticed.

'I just am . . . ' sighed Hannah, 'I'm not really smart or beautiful or a good runner or have anything good about me really . . . just average, I guess . . . ' Hannah fidgeted with her sleeve again, her eyes downcast.

'Well, I know something good about you Hannah,' declared her heart confidently, 'can you guess what it is?'

Hannah wondered briefly if her heart was just teasing her like the big boys did sometimes, and felt her face turn red.

'Think for a moment Hannah, no rush. I know you'll get there eventually,' her heart said gently. Of course, being her heart, it knew what she was thinking and wanted her to know that it was not and never would tease her.

Hannah thought and thought, twirling her brown curls as she did sometimes when she was concentrating, but she just couldn't come up with anything that was good about her. Hot tears welled up in her eyes and she tried hard to gulp down the lump in her throat. She so wished she had something special about her like all the others seemed to have.

'Hannah, you have a good . . . something . . . take a guess then . . . ' prompted her heart, trying to give her a clue.

'Um . . . bike?' said Hannah, hopefully.

'Nope,' replied her heart, patiently.

'Um . . . doll's house?' Hannah suggested, wrinkling her nose at such a silly guess.

'Nope,' said her heart (a little less patiently, Hannah thought to herself, but wasn't quite sure).

'Err . . . party dress?' she said, knowing it was wrong, but she liked mentioning it because she loved that dress, all pink and frilly and bows everywhere.

'Hannah, what am I, chopped liver?' exclaimed her heart, with a touch of exasperation, but laughing at the same time. (The heart made a mental note to apologise to the liver later.)

'The answer is heart, Hannah, heart. You have a good heart!'

'I do?' Hannah said, brightening. Hannah had never thought about that before.

'Hey, trust me, I know you do, Hannah. I'm it!' giggled her heart. 'For instance, do you remember when Melissa fell and you helped her the other day when everyone else was laughing?'

'Yes,' said Hannah, clenching her tiny fists at the thought of it. 'I was mad at them for that. She was hurt.'

'And you wiped her tears away, bandaged her sore knee up with your handkerchief, gave her a cuddle, then took her to see the nurse, waited with her to make sure she was OK . . . ' Her heart took a big breath. That was a long speech, after all. ' . . . And because you did all that you missed your lunch, didn't you? Correct?' reminded her heart.

'Yes I did, but it didn't matter really. I wasn't that hungry, so it was no big deal,' shrugged Hannah, drawing her knees up under her chin. Suddenly it seemed that the stripes on her pyjama sleeves were really interesting to her as she traced their outline up and down with her small fingers. Her heart smiled at this.

'But Hannah, don't you see?' said her heart, 'it did matter. You took the time to help. It mattered to you enough to help Melissa when she was hurt, and I can tell you that it certainly mattered to Melissa that you did.' The voice of her heart became even softer still. 'Listen very carefully to me Hannah, please. Don't ever think that you are ordinary, just because you can't do some things as well as others or because you think they are smarter or prettier or whatever than you. There's no such thing as ordinary. Everyone is special, and has a gift of one kind or another. Yours, my dear Hannah, is that you have a good heart. That is your special gift, you see. Even if I do say so myself, a good heart will take you further in this world than you could ever dream of. So you keep listening to me and you'll do just fine!' declared her heart.

Hannah felt her heart swell inside her chest, puffed up with a warm, fuzzy feeling she would have found hard to describe. Giggling, she snuggled under the warmth of the covers. 'OK, sounds good to me,' she said, grinning widely as she realised that she was special after all and had been all along.

The stars twinkled bigger and brighter than she had ever seen them before as she gazed at them from her pillow, but maybe that was just because her pale blue eyes were shining with happiness. Hannah felt her eyes starting to close as she drifted towards sleep.

'Oh, one last thing before I go, don't worry about the test tomorrow Hannah!' exclaimed her heart.

'Why not?' asked Hannah into the darkness.

'Because I think one little girl might be having to get a special presentation tomorrow for being so thoughtful, and it'll be at the same time as the test,' whispered her heart. If it had hands, her heart would have been clapping them together with excitement. (It just jiggled the valves a bit instead).

'Who?' said Hannah, sitting straight back up again, wide awake, knowing that her heart must mean her, but just wanting to tease a little.

'Sheesh . . . ' joked her heart, of course, knowing that she knew really, but playing along with her game. Hannah and her heart's mingled laughter drifted away on the night air as she fell into a deep, contented sleep, both of them sure they would talk again.

MR NOBODY
Ena Andrews

One day last summer the sky came over very dark and suddenly there was a cloudburst, and to Carena's surprise, there in the garden was a puddle of water with a bright yellow light around it. In fact, it looked just like a big bubble.'

'Look Mummy,' she called, 'there is a big bubble in the garden.'

But Mummy was busy in the kitchen and did not hear.

Carena put on her wellies and went into the garden. There, to her surprise, in the middle of the bubble was a little man, no more than four inches tall. He had a very high-pitched voice. 'Hello there,' he called up to Carena. 'I have just fallen from that big cloud in the sky, and I do not know where I am?'

'Well,' said Carena, 'you have fallen into my garden where I live with my mummy and daddy and my brother James. Anyway, who are you?' she asked.

'I am Nobody,' said the little fellow.

'But you must be somebody,' Carena said.

'I am,' he replied sounding rather cross, 'I am Nobody, and before you ask me, my country is Nowhere.'

'Oh please, don't be silly,' said Carena, 'you must be somebody from somewhere.'

'Now listen little girl,' said Mr Nobody, 'what's your name?'

'I am Carena.'

'Well, if you are Carena, and I believe you, why not believe I am Nobody and I come from Nowhere, eh?'

Carena just stood there with her mouth agape. 'Well I never did!' she exclaimed.

'Of course you didn't,' said Mr Nobody, 'I did.' And with this remark they both started to laugh.

Carena's mummy heard their laughter and went into the garden. 'What are you laughing at?' she asked Carena . . . and then caught sight of the little fellow. 'Well,' she said in surprise at seeing such a little man and standing in a big puddle, right there in the garden. 'Who are you and where did you come from?'

'Here we go again,' said Mr Nobody, and tried to explain to Carena's mummy that he was Nobody from Nowhere. This really did take some understanding, but Mr Nobody said he had to be off and would call there again and see Carena, then left Carena to explain to her mummy.

'Bye for now little Carena,' he called out. 'One day I'll come and see you again,' and then very suddenly the puddle dried up and Mr Nobody was gone and then the yellow light seemed to go into the sky again.

INFORMATION

We hope you have enjoyed reading this book - and that you will continue to enjoy it in the coming years.

If you are interested in becoming a New Fiction author then drop us a line, or give us a call, and we'll send you a free information pack.

Alternatively if you would like to order further copies of this book or any of our other titles, then please give us a call or log onto our website at www.forwardpress.co.uk

**New Fiction Information
Remus House
Coltsfoot Drive
Peterborough
PE2 9JX
(01733) 898101**